# In the Image of His God

## The Curse of the Shroud

PJ Shield

Outskirts Press, Inc.
Denver, Colorado

This is a work of fiction. The events and characters described herein are imaginary and are not intended to refer to specific places or living persons. The opinions expressed in this manuscript are solely the opinions of the author and do not represent the opinions or thoughts of the publisher. The author has represented and warranted full ownership and/or legal right to publish all the materials in this book.

In the Image of His God
The Curse of the Shroud
All Rights Reserved.
Copyright © 2008 PJ Shield
V2.0

Cover Photo © 2008 JupiterImages Corporation. All rights reserved - used with permission.

This book may not be reproduced, transmitted, or stored in whole or in part by any means, including graphic, electronic, or mechanical without the express written consent of the publisher except in the case of brief quotations embodied in critical articles and reviews.

Outskirts Press, Inc.
http://www.outskirtspress.com

ISBN: 978-1-4327-2878-6

Outskirts Press and the "OP" logo are trademarks belonging to Outskirts Press, Inc.

PRINTED IN THE UNITED STATES OF AMERICA

# Dedication

This book is dedicated to all who have helped me on my incredible journey through life. To the darling mother of all my children June, and all my children and grandchildren who reside in Australia and who were at my side during the exciting years in Malta during the 50's.

To Rose whom I excavated in Malta on my return there in 2006, and is my present companion.

To my dear friend Fr. Victor J. Camilleri MSSP, who to this day still continues to build on his amazing legacy at St. Agathas. Malta.

And to fellow Photographer Barrie M. Schwortz, who has inspired my continuing interest in this most sacred relic, through his remarkable web site http://shroud.com. And without who's blessing this work would not have been possible.

"In researching his program, he (Peter) came across www.shroud.com , and got in touch with me by telephone and invited me to appear on his program the following week to help bring his listeners up to date on what was happening since his original interviews. He was kind enough to send me an advance copy of his 1987 interview tape and

*I was immediately overwhelmed at the wonderful historical document I held in my hand.*

*After the program, we again talked about the interview tapes, which I was anxious to archive and share with the Shroud World. Peter immediately and graciously agree to let me remaster the programs and release them all on CD audio....I hope you enjoy them and find them as fascinating as I did."* - **Barrie M. Schwortz**

Finally to those who made my recordings possible and are no longer with us:

*Fr. Peter Rinaldi*
*<u>February 24, 1993:</u> (Ash Wednesday) Because of the repairs to the Royal Chapel, the Shroud, without being taken out of its casket, is removed from its normal shrine in the Royal Chapel and transferred to a specially designed but temporary plate glass display case behind the High Altar, in the main body of Turin Cathedral. In poor health, Fr. Peter Rinaldi has flown from the States to be present at this transfer, but collapses and is taken to a Turin hospital.*

*<u>February 28, 1993:</u> Death of Fr. Peter Rinaldi, one of the co-founders of the Holy Shroud Guild and, along with Frs. Adam Otterbein and Francis Filas, among the main people responsible for helping STURP obtain permission to perform their examination of the Shroud in 1978.*

*June 10$^{th}$ 2000 Dr. Alan Adler*
*July 10$^{th}$ 2002 Walter McCrone*
*March 8$^{th}$, 2005 Raymond N. Rogers (whom I never had the pleasure of meeting)*

*And finally to Roger Dawson, my closest friend for his continuing support.*

*Cover Picture –Dr. Peter J. Shield with Fr. Victor at St. Agathas 1957*

# Preface

Albino Luciani slipped into his satin robe and made his way across his bedroom to where a decanter of wine and a golden goblet had been placed neatly beside his favorite book, Miguel de Cervantes's *Don Quixote*. Albino had read the book from cover to cover at least three times. It helped him relax from the stress and strain of his everyday chores.

He carefully poured himself a measured amount of wine and, taking his book, placed them both on his bedside table before kneeling in silent prayer. Half an hour later he arose, got into his four-poster bed, made himself comfortable and settled back against the array of feather pillows. He picked up his book, took a sip from the goblet and placed it carefully beside him. Thirty seconds later he was engulfed in excruciating pain. The book fell to the floor. The following morning the goblet, the book and the decanter of wine had vanished.

The date was 28 September 1978. Albino Luciani, Pope John Paul I, was dead, a mere thirty-three days after he assumed office. Nineteen days later, a plume of white smoke issued from the Vatican chimney symbolizing the election of a new pontiff.

If John Peters's research had been correct, this would be yet another number added to the list of unexplained deaths to have befallen those who had come in contact with Christendom's most sacred relic, the Holy Shroud of Turin.

# Chapter 1
### (Day 1: early afternoon)

John Peters was restless on the flight from Las Vegas to the Mediterranean island of Malta. He could not get Father Victor's letter out of his mind. It had been over fifty years since John and Victor had last met face to face. Father Victor was now the curator at St. Agatha's Catacombs and Museum. Like John, he was now in his seventies, and much had happened to them both over the ensuing years since they had started excavation on the site.

John had been a freelance photographer working for Associated Press when he was assigned to accompany Cambridge University's archaeological team on the dig. At the time, he had been commissioned by the Maltese government to record all the art and other archaeological treasures that were stored in churches and archives across the Maltese Islands of Malta and Gozo. For nearly five years, John had worked alongside Victor, the novice priest assigned by the missionary order of St. Peter and St. Paul, whose monastery was located above St. Agatha's Crypt and Catacombs. Victor and John had become close friends, a bond that had lasted over the years, supported by occasional communication and the usual birthday and holiday greetings.

After leaving Malta in the mid-'50s, John had returned to Cambridge to teach photography to archaeological students and, after a few years in Ireland, eventually ended up moving to Australia.

Australia had been good for John, and his background with the Archaeological Department at Cambridge University gave him the credentials to launch a career in broadcasting that would last some forty years. Initially, he produced a series of three-minute shorts for radio, which eventually evolved into a television series on mysteries from around the world, both archaeological and occult. In 1987 John was hosting a two-hour Saturday night program for radio station 2CH in Sydney, Australia. Among his guests, via telephone from around the globe, were members of a scientific team labeled the STURP group (Shroud of Turin Research Project), brought together by the US-based Brooks Institute to travel to Turin, Italy, and carry out a series of scientific tests on one of Christendom's most venerated artifacts – the Shroud of Turin, the cloth in which Christ was said to have been wrapped following his crucifixion, before being laid to rest in the tomb, according to Jewish tradition, two days prior to his ascension.

The Shroud had always held a fascination for John because of the unique, inexplicable composition of the image. There had been no explanation for the fact that the image on the cloth appeared as if in a photograph negative. This startling discovery was made on 28 May 1898 when, following a public exhibition, Secondo Pia, an Italian amateur photographer, took the first photograph of the Shroud of Turin. Thus began a new era of scientific research.

When Secondo Pia was developing that first commissioned photograph of this most venerated object, he was stunned to witness the first and only recorded image of the face of Christ as it appeared in the tray of solution before him. What he had photographed was a negative that now appeared in the positive form in his developer tray. Since that date in 1898, the world had been fascinated with this remarkable image and the cloth that the Church only allowed to be exhibited once every twenty-five years. When it had been exhibited to the general public in 1978, millions stood in line for hours just for a glimpse of this miraculous cloth. Since then, the Shroud had been exhibited in 1998 to commemorate the 500th anniversary of the consecration of the Turin Cathedral, and in 2000. The next public exhibition was scheduled in the year 2025.

One by one, John interviewed and interrogated the individual members of the STURP group in a series of interviews over two successive nights. Their opinion was almost unanimous. All but one of the scientific investigative team was convinced that the cloth was all that the Church and historians claimed it to be – the actual burial cloth of Christ.

This was the official finding, despite the fact that they were unable to explain the manner in which this remarkable image had been recorded in negative form on the Shroud.

John was aware that Father Victor had obtained a copy of these now famous interviews which had recently been digitally re-mastered and made available to collectors via one of the team's members, Barrie Schwortz, whose website at http://shroud.com is now recognized as the definitive source for information on the Shroud.

Father Victor, it appeared, had a personal connection with the Shroud, and probably held the answer to what had puzzled the world of Shroud followers and believers since1988, when the cloth had been subjected to carbon dating. The result had conclusively shown the material to have a carbon date of between 1200 and 1500 A.D., ruling out any possibility that it had once held the body of the Savior.

How, John – and millions of believers – wondered, could a group of esteemed scientists have got it so wrong?

The answer to this and the composition of the miraculous image on the cloth were alluded to by Father Victor in his letter to John, which arrived the day before he was to visit Malta to address the members of the recently formed Shroud Society. The group had learned that in the year 1204 A.D., French knights of the Crusader Order of Knights Templar, known as 'the Poor Knights of Christ and of the Temple of Solomon', brought it to France; **on the way they must have stopped**

**at Malta to take fresh water and food.** The Shroud Society planned to hold their annual convention at each of the locations that the Shroud was reported to have visited. Malta was chosen as the first of these. As the keynote speaker at their inaugural convocation, John had been asked to present his lecture on the interview recordings.

\*\*\*

As he settled into his room at the Radisson SAS Hotel at St. Julian's Bay, he wondered what his friend of fifty years, closeted within St. Agatha's, had unearthed that could be of such significant value to his personal investigative studies. Exhausted as he was after his long flight, John found his brain whirling with the facts he was so familiar with. He mentally ticked them off.

At a press conference held in Turin on 13 October 1988, Cardinal Ballestrero, Archbishop of Turin, made an official announcement: the results of the three laboratories performing the carbon dating of the Shroud had determined an approximate date of 1325 A.D. for the cloth.

At a similar press conference held at the British Museum, London, it was announced that the cloth dated back to somewhere between 1260 and 1390 A.D. Newspaper headlines across the world immediately branded the Shroud a fake and, more importantly, declared that the Catholic Church had accepted the results. This was disputed when, on 28 April 1989, Pope John Paul II, being interviewed by journalists on a plane journey during the papal visit to Africa, guardedly spoke of the Shroud as an authentic relic, while insisting that the Church had never taken a formal stand in this regard.

On 30 September of that same year, one of the world's most prestigious scientific publications, *The New Scientist*, reported the findings of the scientific workshop at East Kilbride: "... the margin of error with radiocarbon-dating ... may be two or three times as great as practitioners of the technique have claimed".

Three independent universities had conducted the carbon dating process and all had come up with roughly the same conclusion – that the cloth was no older than 1200 A.D. Even allowing for the recognized margin of error, the cloth originated at the latest in the mid-1500s, at the earliest in the 900s.

In addition to this, according to a recent report that John had read in the scientific journal *Thermochimica Acta*, Raymond N. Rogers, a Fellow of the Los Alamos National Laboratory, claimed the sample tested in 1988 was from a medieval mend in the cloth.

John opened his briefcase and shuffled through his papers to locate the one he wanted. It was headed: **Studies on the radiocarbon sample from the shroud of Turin**

*Raymond N. Rogers Los Alamos National Laboratory, University of California, 1961 Cumbres Patio, Los Alamos, NM 87544, USA Received 14 April 2004; revised 14 April 2004; accepted 12 September 2004. Available online 16 November 2004.*

*That's the one I'm looking for,* John confirmed, as he continued reading:

*Abstract*

*In 1988, radiocarbon laboratories at Arizona, Cambridge, and Zurich determined the age of a sample from the Shroud of Turin. They reported that the date of the cloth's production lay between A.D. 1260 and 1390 with 95% confidence. This came as a surprise in view of the technology used to produce the cloth, its chemical composition, and the lack of vanillin in its lignin. The results prompted questions about the validity of the sample. Preliminary estimates of the kinetics constants for the loss of vanillin from lignin indicate a much older age for the cloth than the radiocarbon analyses. The radiocarbon sampling area is uniquely coated with a yellow-brown plant gum containing dye lakes. Pyrolysis-mass-spectrometry results from the sample area coupled with microscopic and microchemical observations prove that the radiocarbon sample was not part of the original cloth of the Shroud of Turin. The radiocarbon date was thus not valid for determining the true age of the shroud.*

John again found himself wondering how all of this tied in with the intriguing letter from Father Victor. There were so many facts, and no discernable link. What could be important enough for his old friend to contact him so urgently after so many long years?

# Chapter 2
## (Day 1: midafternoon)

John took out Father Victor's letter and, for the umpteenth time, read the carefully worded document:

*27 February 2005*

**Dear John,**

**It has been many years since we last communicated, and much water has passed under both our bridges. It was with great interest that I listened to your recorded interviews with the STURP group. You would of course not be aware, but several years ago fate brought the Shroud and I together under somewhat amazing circumstances. In 1990 I had the pleasure of meeting His Holiness Pope John Paul II and he had remarked on his admiration for the work I have been doing over these many years since your departure, on preserving the ancient treasures that abound here on this tiny island. He confided in me at that time that a plan had been put in place by the papal administration to protect the integrity of the sacred cloth**

and preserve forever this remarkable treasure. He asked for my assistance, which I had no hesitation in giving.

I have recently become worried that a member of my staff here has compromised this secret and urgently need your advice and guidance. I feel sure, in view of our long-standing friendship, that I can rely on your discretion and your advice.

*Please call me as soon you get here, at the number mentioned above, and we can arrange a meeting. I have much to tell you.*

*May God bless you.*

**Sincerely**

And the letter was signed simply *Victor*.

John reached for the phone and dialed the number Victor had given him.

"Minn hemm?"

John immediately recognized Father Victor's voice. "It's John Peters," he answered. "How are you, Victor?"

There was relief in Victor's voice as he recognized his old friend.

"I'm fine – good to hear your voice. I was hoping you'd call."

Cutting through the usual preliminaries, John asked, "When would you like to meet, Victor?"

"As soon as possible." Victor's voice held an undercurrent of urgency.

"I'm free this evening if you wish," John said. "If you prefer, we could meet here in my hotel room. That way, we won't be overheard. I believe the matter you wish to discuss is confidential?" He was wary about even hinting at the subject matter that he knew Victor was anxious to discuss.

Victor was evidently relieved at John's obvious caution.

"That would be great, John. Where are you staying?"

"The Radisson, room number 235. Would 7 o'clock be okay?"

"Thank you, John. That'll be fine."

John hung up and started to unpack, knowing sleep would elude him. It was 4 pm – he had plenty of time to shower and grab a bite. He couldn't imagine what startling news Victor might bring, but he knew from the urgency in his old friend's voice that the matter was both important and critical.

There seemed no logical explanation as to how a missionary priest could have relevant information on any aspect of the Shroud mystery. If, as Father Victor had mentioned, his involvement began with a meeting in 1990 with Pope John Paul II, John needed more information on the man who had become the longest serving Pope in history.

Perhaps some quick research would give him a clue. John opened his laptop and typed: **Pope John Paul II – Malta**.

He read with interest the speech made by His Holiness on his arrival in Malta:

*The memory of my first visit, eleven years ago, spontaneously comes to my mind. I remember my meetings with the priests and religious, the workers, the intellectuals, the families and the young people. I remember the Co-Cathedral of Saint John in Valletta, the Marian Shrines of Mellieha and Ta' Pinu on the Island of Gozo. I remember the Bay and the Islands of Saint Paul, and in particular the ancient Grotto, venerated as the place where he stayed.*

John had been aware of the Pope's deep interest in everything scientific and his support for Catholic scientists. He recalled how his speech before the Pontifical Academy of Sciences on 22 October 1996 had resulted in headlines around the world.

John typed in the new keywords, hit the search button again, and read the pontiff's speech:

### Truth cannot contradict truth

*... For my part, when I received those taking part in your academy's plenary assembly on October 31, 1992, I had the opportunity with regard to Galileo to draw attention to the need of a rigorous hermeneutic for the correct interpretation of the inspired word ...*

*Taking into account the state of scientific research at the time as well as of the requirements of theology, the encyclical 'Humani Generis' considered the doctrine of 'evolutionism' a serious hypothesis, worthy of investigation and in-depth study equal to that of the opposing hypothesis ... Today, almost half a century after the publication of the encyclical, new knowledge has led to the recognition of the theory of evolution as more than a hypothesis ...*

*What is to be decided here is the true role of philosophy and, beyond it, of theology.*

John needed some air. He shut down his laptop and headed for the street. A short walk before he met with Father Victor wouldn't do any harm.

As he strolled down the hill to St. Julian's Bay, he glanced at the towering edifice of Villa Rosa, perched high above the small sandy beach, with its imposing gardens stretching down the bayside. John had fond memories of this majestic property. He and some of his friends had opened a bar for British servicemen there in the '50s. John remembered the gardens with empty animal cages that had once held exotic animals from around the world. Malta was then an integral part of Britain and still occupied by British garrisons. The Airport – Luqa – was the British Air Force staging post for the Middle East. The siege of Malta during World War II had been well documented. The British flag flew proudly over the island for nearly 200 years.

John was tempted to continue his stroll around the bay to Dragonara Palace, though he had read that it was now converted to a five star hotel and casino. It would have to wait. There were more urgent matters at hand. He turned and walked briskly up the hill to his hotel and his reunion with a dear friend.

After a quick shower, John went down to the dining room. Knowing that Malta was famous for its fresh seafood, he ordered salmon, his favorite fish. He was not disappointed. He felt the familiar craving for dessert, but doubting he could do it justice in his present restless mood, decided to tie up a few loose ends instead.

Back in his room, he took a few minutes to contact the convention organizer and set up an appointment to discuss his presentation, scheduled for the closing dinner to be held in three days' time. They agreed to meet the following morning at the breakfast launch to be held at the Mediterranean Convention Center in the heart of Valletta. He also called the curator of the Wignacourt Museum in connection with some restoration work he would be handling on one of the replicas of the Shroud.

That out of the way, John settled back in anticipation to await the friend he hadn't seen in half a century.

# Chapter 3
(Day 1: evening)

The discreet ringing startled John out of a light doze. He opened the door to his old friend.

For a few minutes time stood still as the two men embraced. Their birthdays were separated by only two days and they had often celebrated them together. Despite their closeness in age, there was a marked difference in the ravaging effects of time. Victor's stooped shoulders and thinning hair showed every bit of his 74 years. His pale face looked haunted and, despite his thick glasses, it was clear that he had trouble seeing. John thought that the years underground in the labyrinth of catacombs and crypts had taken a heavy toll on Victor's body. His heart went out to his dear friend.

"You look good, Victor," John said as their warm embrace ended.

"I wish that were so, my friend – the years have not been kind to this tired old body. You, on the other hand, look just as you did fifty years ago!" The two men spontaneously burst into laughter. The brief tension was gone – they were just two friends reunited at last after many long years.

## In the Image of His God

"I've ordered us some wine to mark this occasion," John said. "We've a lot of catching up to do, Victor."

Victor squinted as he examined the label on the bottle. "Ah, Malta Heritage. Splendid! You're right. We have much to discuss."

For the next half hour they briefly discussed their ups and downs on the sea of life and the reasons for John's visit to the island. Victor abruptly brought their conversation back to the matter in hand and the reason he was now in need of his old companion.

"John," said Victor, his voice suddenly taking a somber note. "I have a very serious situation and no one I can turn to. I hope you don't mind me confiding in you, even though we haven't seen each other for so many years. I know I can count on your discretion."

"Of course, Victor, I'm only too pleased to help if I can. I must confess I'm at a loss about exactly how I could possibly be of service, but I'm sure you wouldn't have written the letter you did and arranged such a quick meeting if you did not feel there was something I could do. You have me intrigued, especially if it involves the Shroud. Tell me more!"

From the anxious look on Victor's face, John knew this was no trivial matter.

Victor removed his glasses and polished them slowly, as he met John's eyes. "As you know, my life has been devoted to preserving our treasures from the past. Since we parted fifty years ago, I have spent almost every day in the service of our Lord, locating and preserving, as far as I could, those fragments of our past that lie at our feet everywhere one turns on this small island.

"My work apparently did not go unnoticed, and when Pope John Paul II visited us here in 2001 he was apparently impressed by my efforts. I was amazed to find a message scrawled in his own hand awaiting me on my return to my quarters one day, requesting that I call on him at the Presidential Palace where he was staying. I wondered what His Holiness could possibly want of me."

"That was indeed a great honor! But do go on."

"When I got there, I was ushered into his quarters and he immediately instructed those present to leave and told them that under no circumstances were we to be disturbed. You can imagine the thoughts that went rushing through my brain as this great man beckoned me to be seated next to him. He took my hand and asked if I would join him in prayer. As we knelt together, I couldn't help but be overpowered by his great spirit. There was no doubt in my mind that this was God's disciple on earth." Tears welled up in Victor's eyes as he relived those precious moments. He blinked them back, mopped his brow and put on his glasses, obviously at a loss over how to proceed.

"Go on, Victor," John encouraged, feeling an unbelievable excitement building inside him. It was almost as if he was reliving the moments as Victor described them.

"His Holiness spoke briefly about my devotion to my work and my calling, and said that I had been chosen to help preserve one of the Church's greatest treasures. He explained that what he was about to confide in me was to be a secret that must remain between us and was only known to a very few chosen members of his personal staff. The relic in question was of course, as you've possibly guessed, the Holy Shroud."

Victor took a healthy sip of wine.

"I knew little of the Shroud before that time," he went on. "I knew, of course, of its existence and never for a moment doubted its authenticity, as it was an esteemed relic of the church. On reading on your website of your interviews with the STURP group, I bought the discs and listened with great interest to the findings of the scientists involved. I had the pleasure of meeting Father Peter Rinaldi in Turin at a seminar some years earlier, but didn't know of his role in the preservation of the Shroud."

## In the Image of His God

John thought how pleased he had been with the interview he had done with Father Rinaldi, the man appointed by Rome to be keeper of the holy relic and to whom the Pope was said to have confirmed that the face on the Shroud was that of Christ.

"His Holiness," Victor said, "told me that the Church had been pleased by the results presented by members of the investigative team, despite the one dissenting voice of Walter McCrone. He went on to say, however, that there was serious concern that the cloth would suffer greatly if it were subjected to further tests and exposure. This was heightened by considerable pressure to expose the cloth to the carbon dating process. Segments would have to be cut from the cloth in order for the tests to be carried out – a procedure His Holiness was totally opposed to."

"I can understand why," John muttered.

"So could I," Victor said. "The Pope went on to explain that after much prayer and pondering over this matter, he had concluded that little would be proved by carbon dating verification. He, members of the Church, and now the STURP team, all knew full well that this was the cloth in which the Savior had been wrapped at the time his body had been placed in the tomb. This relic is now truly one of the gospels, the only real evidence that Christ suffered in the manner the writings of the disciples had stated. Contact with the Shroud is as close as one can come to touching Christ himself!"

He paused, as if uncertain how to continue. "The Pope reasoned that if the carbon dating were to show the cloth to be other than a first-century relic, there would still be no explanation for the remarkable image or how it got there. There would still be those who would insist on further tests. If, for whatever reason, the tests showed that the cloth were to be of *a much later period*, this would do little to shake the faith of the true believers ... however, His Holiness felt that it would put an end to such tests if those of little faith were satisfied that it was indeed a fake."

Victor paused to sip his wine. John listened in amazement. He had heard rumors of the Pope's intense interest in the Shroud. Still, he could hardly believe what he was hearing from this old friend seated before him.

"You know, Victor," he said thoughtfully, "Father Rinaldi mentioned an occasion when he was in the presence of His Holiness. He told me that the Pope had turned to him, pointing to the face on the Shroud, and said in hushed tones, 'Whenever I look on this face, I know I am looking at Him – it is the Lord!' I thought at the time that this was an amazing admission from one who so many believe speaks for God."

Victor nodded slowly, in unspoken consent. "His Holiness proceeded to explain to me that after much contemplation and prayer it had been decided that this most holy relic be removed from public display and any further possible harm. The dilemma arose as to how to explain this without appearing to be afraid of the outcome of further tests. A number of scenarios were contemplated and discussed, until it was suggested that the Church replace the original with a 'true fake' and –"

"Wait a minute," John interrupted. What do you mean by a 'true fake'? A replica?"

"Well, word had reached Father Rinaldi that an actual copy of the original, almost indistinguishable from the real one, had been made by none other than Leonardo da Vinci, whilst he served as Grand Master of the Priory of Sion," Victor explained. "The Pope told me that Father Rinaldi had undertaken the task of finding this copy to replace the actual Shroud in the cathedral in Turin. The original was to be brought to His Holiness at the Vatican for safekeeping."

John sat absolutely still, dumfounded. He could hardly believe his ears. Here, at last, was the explanation for all his misgivings. How had the STURP team got it so wrong? The simple explanation was that they hadn't! But Leonardo da Vinci? John knew there was a series of replica shrouds in existence – about thirty-eight in all, as far as he knew. In fact, he was scheduled to undertake the restoration of one of them this week. It was housed in the Wignacourt Museum in

# In the Image of His God

the same city as Father Victor's St. Agatha's Catacombs – Rabat.

Whenever such a reproduction was obtained, John recalled, the Shroud was held in veneration by the faithful. He knew of such reproductions in several countries: there is one in Belgium and another in Argentina; two in France and two others in Portugal; thirteen in Spain and nineteen in Italy, besides the original Shroud of Turin.

Apart from the Shroud of Rabat, another of these reproductions, held in Spain, was of particular interest to him, as he had had the opportunity some years ago to visit it. It was obtained through the good offices of a Grand Prior of the Knights of Malta.

Francisco Lucas Bueno, Bishop of Malta and Grand Master of the Religion of St. John in the year 1650 A.D., obtained a copy from the Royal Savoy Family. On 8 October 1652, he sent the Shroud to Saragossa to the Lord Receiver of St. John who, in turn, entrusted it to Antonio Bueno and Andres Martinez of Campillo de Aragon. They gave it to the people of Campillo. This relic, John recalled, is kept over the altar in a chapel constructed for the purpose and is guarded by two strong doors in gold.

Victor had been closely watching John's face for a reaction as he unfolded the events of that dramatic first meeting with his beloved pontiff. He noticed the look of total amazement on John's face switch to one of almost total disbelief.

"I know how incredible all this must seem to you, John, particularly as you've been so close to the investigative work that has been carried out. It's why I felt that, in light of the disaster I am about to unfold, you were just about the only person I could trust with the true facts."

"I think this calls for a top-up," John said, reaching for the bottle of wine and refilling their glasses. "Please continue, Victor."

"I must confess that I was not prepared for what followed. His Holiness rose from his chair and walked toward a silver casket placed on the coffee table in front of him. To my continuing amazement, he opened the box and carefully displayed the contents. There before me was the holy relic – the burial cloth of Christ! I dropped to my knees, overcome with uncontrollable emotion." Victor paused, as if unable to continue. His eyes blurred with unshed tears.

John felt a prickle of alarm. Victor was obviously under deep emotional stress. *What could possibly be worrying him so?* he wondered. He was soon to find out.

# Chapter 4
(Day 1: late evening)

"Victor, my dear friend," John said soothingly, moving across and placing a comforting arm around Victor's shoulder. "I can understand how overwhelmed you must have been."

Victor removed his glasses and fumbled for a handkerchief to wipe his eyes.

With obvious effort, he continued. "His Holiness told me that after much contemplation he had personally selected me and the island of Malta to safeguard this remarkable treasure. Having withstood the onslaught of many nations and been home to the Knights Templar, there was no better fortress than this to protect this most Holy of Holies. He had even selected the location! The sacred grotto of St. Paul. As I'm sure you're aware, St. Paul and St. Luke were prisoners on their way to Rome to be tried for political rebellion, when their ship floundered on the rocky coast of Malta, somewhere to the north of St. Paul's Bay. They sheltered for the winter in a cave near Rabat and were cared for by the locals who, as the apostle recorded, were renowned for their hospitality."

John recalled the speech made by the Pope on his second visit to the island in 2001, when he had specifically mentioned the sacred grotto. In a speech that had been widely reported, the Pope had said:

*I remember the Bay and the Islands of Saint Paul, and in particular the ancient Grotto, venerated as the place where he stayed.*

"You mean to tell me, Victor, that the actual Shroud is right *here*, on the island?" John gasped, his mind reeling under this incredible news.

"Well … that, my dear friend, is just the problem. I don't know!"

Noticing the bewildered look on John's face, he hastened to explain. "You see, ten days ago the Shroud vanished. I was the only one on the island who knew the whereabouts of the precious cloth, or so I thought. As I didn't want to draw attention to my interest in it or my close inspection of it, I would secretly visit its location once a week to check on its safety. Ten days ago, I went as usual and to my utter amazement and dismay the casket was … was gone."

Victor looked at John with haunted eyes. "I had no idea what to do – the possibility that someone would steal it seemed almost impossible. It was not a situation I had ever considered. Who could I tell without disclosing to the world that the real Shroud not only actually existed but that the Church had purposely misled the investigation? His Holiness placed his trust in me and I … I have failed." His voice broke.

Making an obvious effort to control himself, Victor cleared his throat and gave John a tired smile. "When I read that you were to visit the island, my heart leapt with hope. Here was someone I could confide in without letting the cat out of the bag, so to speak. You will help me won't you, John?" Victor's eyes pleaded far louder than his words.

John was struggling to come to terms with what he had just heard. Over the last few days, since he had received Victor's letter, he could not have conceived of an event of such magnitude in his wildest imagination. He fully understood the total devastation that Victor must have felt. The frustration of having no one to tell or call on for help ... his heart reached out to his friend.

"My dear Victor, of course I'll do whatever I can, though I'm at a total loss about where to start. Perhaps you should start by telling me just where exactly it was placed and who could possibly have had access to the location. I'm sure you must have some idea. Are you up to discussing it tonight or would you rather reconvene in the morning?"

Victor looked on the verge of collapse – though there was no doubt that having John to share his burden had lightened his load considerably. Perhaps a good night's rest would benefit them both.

"I have a breakfast appointment in Valetta first thing in the morning – what say we meet at around 11 am? I could drive over to St. Agatha's and we can make our plans then," John suggested.

As he rose to leave, Victor embraced his old friend. "Thank you, John. I believe God has sent you to me in my hour of need. 11 am will be fine – do you think you can remember the way?"

John chuckled, "I certainly hope so, Victor. After all it has only been fifty years!"

Neither would get much sleep that night.

# Chapter 5
(Day 2: morning)

John arrived early at the Mediterranean Conference Center. His key-note speech was the last thing on his mind. The convention organizer introduced him to the assembled gathering and John received a warm round of applause from everyone present. As Shroud buffs, they were well conversant with the work John had done in bringing the story of this remarkable cloth to the public through his radio and television programs. There was little doubt they would all be in at-tendance when John next appeared before them. He briefed the tech-nical staff on his audio-visual requirements for the dinner, had a brief chat with the American Ambassador, and hastily left for the car park where his rented car awaited him.

The drive to Rabat held many memories for John. How well he recalled his fascination with the stone-walled dirt roads, with grazing sheep and an abundance of prickly pears on either side. In particular, he recalled one fine sunny afternoon when he had impulsively jumped from his car to photograph a young shepherdess as she sat tending her flock. She was stunning, and John had felt an immediate physical attraction. He would long remember the sweetness of her lips, though he never saw her after that idyllic day. *It's funny,* he thought. *After fifty years, and more romantic encounters than I could possibly remember – many of which took place on this tiny island – and several that lasted months and even years, I've never forgotten that passionate sun-drenched afternoon with a simple farm girl who hardly spoke my language ... It's probably one of the many reasons I love this place.*

As he followed the newly paved road towards the walled city of M'dina, the ancient capital of this multicultural island, he thought of the tremendous history that had engulfed the shores of this tiny Mediterranean enclave. Sitting as Malta does in the center of the Mediterranean, it has been colonized and invaded repeatedly since man first discovered the art of boat building. Until it became independent in 1964, Malta had been occupied at different times by the Phoenicians, Carthaginians, Romans, Byzantines, Arabs, Normans, Germans, Spaniards, crusading Knights, the French and eventually the British, whose inimitable mark remains indelibly stamped on Malta.

Over 7,000 years ago, around 5500 B.C., the first settlers found their way from Sicily and settled in caves, the remains of which are still visible today. Fossilized remains date back 125,000 years. The oldest known standing man-made structure in the world is neither Stonehenge nor the Pyramids, but the temple at G'gantija, on the neighboring island of Gozo. Surely no country, large or small, could compete with Malta for sheer historic content.

Every civilization from the early Phoenicians to the more recent British had left their indelible mark on the architecture and culture of this tiny isolated world. The Knights Templar had fortified the harbors, built palaces and left their signature all over the islands. John could almost hear the clash of swords and the screams of men dying in battle, in a land far from their homes.

The ancient walled capital of M'dina loomed before him. He recalled a legend, told to him long ago by Father Victor, of the terrible siege of this city in 1565. Since then, he had made it a point to learn more.

The Knights of Jerusalem had been in possession of the island for over thirty years when, in 1565, Suleyman, the mighty Turk who earned the title of 'the Magnificent' for his exploits and personal qualities, sent a great army to seize Malta and to suppress the Order of St. John, which had become a serious obstacle to the Ottoman Empire. But the Knights, under the inspiring and brave leadership of their Grand Master, Father Jean de La Valette, a Provencal, heroically resisted the formidable attack of the Turkish army. The defenders even placed a statue of their beloved St. Agatha on the bastion walls to protect them against the overwhelming onslaught of the Turks. The shattered and dispirited Ottomans finally left the island on 13 September 1565 – a victory still commemorated by the Maltese.

Following the lifting of the siege, the defenses of the island were in a very poor state. Members of the Order, fearing another Turkish attack, were in favor of relinquishing the island. La Valette, however, was convinced that the Order should not leave. He was determined to build a new city in Malta, so strong that it could defy the powers of the Infidels, and so beautiful that it would be a fit abode for the glorious and illustrious Order. Valletta became the island's capital in 1571 and M'dina became the Silent City it is today.

Reflecting on the richness of the island's history, John wound his way through the narrow streets of Rabat. As he entered the town square in front of the imposing St. Paul's Church, he was brought almost to a standstill as busloads of tourists flocked through the narrow streets to visit the crypt of St. Paul and St. Peter and St. Paul's Catacombs. Most of them, led by government appointed guides, were unaware that a few meters opposite lay the far more impressive St. Agatha's Crypt and Catacombs, and the unique museum maintained by the Missionary Society of St. Paul. The stunning frescoes that adorned the walls of the crypt and the Sancta Sanctorum, and the skeleton remains of some of the original inhabitants, made a visit to St. Agatha's the experience of a lifetime. From what Victor had discussed last evening, John was aware that, over the last fifty years, the priest had created an amazing collection of not only treasures from the crypt and catacombs below, but from around the Mediterranean basin, including all of the Maltese archaeological sites.

John drove cautiously down the one-way street, Hal Bajjada, tucked away as it is in the narrow streets of Rabat, opposite St. Paul's Catacombs. In his opinion as an archaeologist, though St. Paul's Catacombs was the most famous tourist site in Malta, there was no comparison with the Crypt of St. Agatha. Victor, John believed, was unquestionably one of the most knowledgeable authorities on the ancient catacombs. He more than deserved to be the present curator of the amazing museum he had created at St. Agatha's.

From John's own early work at the site, there was little doubt in his mind that the frescoes of St. Agatha's were the finest in Malta. As he parked his car in the only remaining spot, John thought of the unforgettable day he and Victor broke through the rubble and discovered what is now considered Malta's first church.

The Sancta Sanctorum, Malta's first church, is believed to have been located in the catacombs. The Maltese catacombs were never meant to be hiding places during persecutions, nor were they intended to be living quarters. They were underground cemeteries consisting of long, narrow corridors with tombs on each side, and vaults. Some of the tombs are also decorated with reliefs and frescoes.

Most of the tombs were used for the internment of two people. Sometimes, a double tomb has a thin wall separating one from the other. At times the tombs are side by side, and not only two, but even three, four or five persons were buried in the same grave.

Almost all the graves have headrests in the form of rock pillows. In each grave there is a semicircular cavity where the head of the deceased person was rested. These cavities indicate the number of people buried in each grave.

One of the most remarkable features that they had discovered in the Maltese catacombs was the 'agape table', probably used as a table for the final farewell repast. This is a round table hewn out of live rock, about 2 feet or more above ground level. As archaeological features, agape tables usually slope gently downwards toward the circumference of the chamber. At the upper end they form a round table, flat and encircled with a rim about 2.4 inches wide and 1.2 inches high. Generally, these tables are about 2.5 feet in diameter. At the front of the table, a small section of the rim is left open. John had concluded that this served to clean and wash the table when the meal was over.

Two of the tombs in St. Agatha's Catacombs are decorated with mural paintings. On the wall near the head of one of these tombs, there is a Greek inscription: 'Before the Calends of September, Leonias was buried here'. This inscription has suffered through negligence over the years and is difficult to read.

The other tomb, as John remembered, is a table grave, and is decorated with frescoes that were hidden under a layer of nearly 2.5 inches of mortar. A colored frieze goes round the edges, while a pelican in red ochre is seen on each side. On the inner sides, there are floral wreathes with pink roses and green leaves, with three roses in the center of each wreath. It seemed likely that on the back of the grave there were more frescoes which, when John had last been there, still lay hidden under more mortar.

John felt a pleasant tingle of excitement at the thought of re-visiting a place that had been so much a part of his early life, and had such a significant impact on his future.

# Chapter 6
## (Day 2: midmorning)

As he locked the car and headed for St. Agatha's, John recalled the numerous occasions he had walked the walled pathway leading to the crypt entrance and the Society's complex. The Missionary Society of St. Peter and St. Paul ran a very prestigious boys' school. Many students from the school chose to join the Order and assume teaching roles around the world.

He immediately saw his old friend awaiting him at the top of the crypt steps. Though deep lines creased Victor's face, John could see he was making an effort to be welcoming.

"How wonderful to be back after all these years, Victor," John said in greeting. "It's obvious you've not been idle while I've been gone."

"Come," said Victor, taking John's arm. "Let me show you around."

They descended the steps leading down to St. Agatha's Crypt. John was amazed at the remarkable work that had been done since his departure in 1960, to preserve the original frescoes that adorned the walls and altar, many dating back to 600 A.D.

Victor said, "As you may recall, in the acts of the pastoral visit by Monsignor Pietro Duzina in 1575, it was recorded that there were many altars in the crypt. Nowadays, as you see, only two remain. The main altar and a side altar dedicated to Our Lady, Mother of Divine Grace."

John gazed around him, feeling the familiar sensation of reverential awe. The crypt of St. Agatha is hewn out of live rock. It is an underground basilica which, from the early ages, was venerated by the Maltese. At the time of St. Agatha's stay, the crypt was a small natural cave, which later on, during the fourth or fifth century, was enlarged and embellished. At the far end of the crypt, there is the main altar dedicated to the Saint. Till 1647, this altar was still used for worship.

When Monsignor Lucas Buenos was bishop of Malta from 1664 to 1668 A.D., he visited this sacred place, and donated to the crypt an alabaster statue, representing the saint undergoing her martyrdom.

It is a fine work of art, sculptured in Trapani, and represents the Saint tied to a tree trunk, with a cherub holding a crown of roses over her head. Both breasts have been severed from her body. The statue is set on a baroque pedestal within which there is a tiny statue of the Saint, depicting her set on fire. John remembered it had held pride of place at the center of the altar. In its place, John noticed a new fiberglass statue of the saint.

"What happened to St. Agatha?" John enquired. "You've replaced her with another statue?"

"She was far too precious to leave down here; I've given her the protection she deserves."

"And where did you get this one? It's obviously quite contemporary."

"This one's the work of the Maltese artist, Anton Agius," Victor said. "Nowadays, the original statue resides in the museum upstairs. I thought we would talk there after you've had an opportunity to renew your acquaintance with your old stomping ground." John was amused by Victor's turn of phrase, and very relieved to hear the familiar banter despite the priest's predicament.

Sensing John's deep interest, Victor gently touched his shoulder. "Why don't you take a few minutes to explore, and I'll go and tell the attendants that we're not to be disturbed."

John was grateful to Victor for the chance to re-explore a project that had meant so much to him and been so influential in shaping his career. It was the overwhelming desire to bring such incredible treasures as this crypt to the attention of an ever-hungry traveling public that had led John away from this initial career into radio and television all those years ago. John's first radio program had recounted the story of St. Agatha.

According to legend, during the Roman Emperor Trajanus Decius's persecution, in the years 249 to 251 A.D., Agatha and some of her friends fled from Sicily, her native land, and took refuge in Malta.

Some historians believe that her stay on the island was rather short, and she spent her days there in the crypt at Rabat in prayer, teaching the Christian faith to the children. After some time, Agatha realized that it would be better for her to return to her native land and practice her faith there, even at the risk of martyrdom.

On landing in Sicily, Agatha was arrested and brought before Quintanus, praetor of Catania, who condemned her to torture and imprisonment. Her breasts were severed from her body. After a few days, on 5 February 251, she died in prison as a martyr. The crypt where she used to pray was named after her, as were the nearby catacombs and, later on, the church now located over the crypt.

The catacombs were John's main area of interest. He recalled the photographs he had taken, the sheer thrill of uncovering each hidden treasure. Who knew what further mysteries lay buried within?

As he made his way to the entrance to the catacombs, he vividly remembered how they had crawled on hands and knees through these underground tunnels holding kerosene lamps as they removed hundreds of years of rubble from within the tombs. Now, thanks to Victor and his team's efforts, small electric lights illuminated every corner of the labyrinth of tunnels and graves. Over two-thirds of the catacombs were out of bounds to tourists. How often, John reminisced, he had been lost in complete darkness in the miles of passages until Victor showed him how to find his way out?

As he entered the Sancta Sanctorum, he recalled the excitement they had all felt as they slowly and painstakingly removed the layers of rubble and mold that had concealed this treasure for centuries. The Sancta Sanctorum has a radius of just over 9 feet and is decorated with a pillar on each side. There is a capstone on top of the pillars, which are joined by a frieze that goes all round the chamber. On one side there is an arch, which was the altar of this primitive chapel. It is decorated with a third-century fresco representing a scallop shell, painted in various colors: red ochre, dark green, yellow and pale yellow.

The front lintel is painted in dark red and dark brown. It symbolizes the source of life that is God. In the middle there is a cross with the Greek letter *rho* with a horizontal line passing through its middle, an artistic variation of the Greek letter *chi*, symbolizing Christ. On the ends of the horizontal line, there are the Greek letters *alpha* and *omega*, which signify that Christ is the beginning and the end of life. Apart from the flowers, on both sides of the fresco, there is a dove with leaves or flowers in its claws. Gazing at it, John thought this was probably the best fresco that existed in the catacombs and it probably belonged to the earliest age of the Christian era.

"Are you there, John?" he heard Father Victor call out.

"Yes, Victor – need you ask where?" Their easy camaraderie had been one of John's fondest memories of their thrilling discoveries. He turned and saw Victor's stooped figure approaching through the narrow entrance.

## In the Image of His God

"I knew I'd find you here," Victor chuckled. "Let's move to my office in the museum. I've left instructions that we're not to be disturbed." The old priest slowly led the way back down the passages to the crypt and up the stairs to where the museum was housed.

"My God, Victor!" John gasped, as he followed his friend into the museum. "Where on earth did you find all this amazing stuff?"

"It's been my life's work, John." Victor was obviously and rightly proud, John thought, of what he had achieved.

"This is incredible!" John said, staring around him. "No wonder His Holiness was impressed!"

John's mention of the pontiff suddenly jolted both men back to the terrible plight that lay before them. The missing Holy Shroud of Turin.

They entered Victor's small office, which was strewn with books, manuscripts, boxes of coins and numerous artifacts still to be cataloged.

"Make yourself comfortable, John," said Victor, moving to a small armchair and removing a pile of books that looked like they had been there forever. He pulled his chair from behind his desk and sat beside John.

"Okay," John said. "Start at the beginning and tell me everything that has happened since you took possession of the silver casket."

For the next three hours Victor told John of the events following his meeting with the Pope. The silver casket His Holiness had shown him had been delivered to his St. Agatha office by a Vatican guard. He had noted that the casket was accompanied by a re-sealed letter of obvious antiquity. The letter was in the unmistakable hand of none other than Leonardo da Vinci himself. It had been written supposedly in his last hours, telling of the replica shroud he had created and claiming that he had changed the face to resemble his own. It was the discovery of this letter by Father Rinaldi that had led to the idea that here was a suitable substitute to take the place of the sacred relic in the eventual swap prior to the carbon dating.

His Holiness had been quite specific as to exactly where the locked silver casket should be stored.

"I have remembered and treasured what His Holiness said to me that day. I can recall every word clearly," Victor said. "I keep thinking about those words…"

"Go on, Victor. Tell me what he said," John urged.

"His Holiness said 'I was, as you are aware, Father, deeply moved and inspired in the grotto where our beloved St. Paul had sheltered during his mission here. It is here at the feet of this likeness that I wish the Shroud to rest'.

"He went on to say, 'St. Paul had a profound effect on the development of Christian theology, including promulgation of the concepts of redemption through faith in Christ, the abrogation of the old Law and the beginning of the age of the Spirit, Christ as the eternal Son of God, His pre-existence before the Incarnation, His exaltation to God's right hand after the Resurrection, the Church as the mystical Body of Christ, and the belief that Christians live in Christ and will eventually be transformed at the final resurrection. I believe the spirit of St. Paul still abides there, and I can think of no more fitting location for all that remains of our dear departed Jesus Christ to repose'," Victor quoted, his voice thickening with emotion.

"'But, Your Holiness, thousands of people visit the grotto each year and security is minimal', I pointed out. But he would have none of it."

"The Pope must have had his reasons for choosing the grotto. But surely some security measures were put in place?" John asked.

"Prior to the arrival of the silver casket, I again visited the sacred grotto to see how best I could comply with His Holiness's wishes. I contacted the present curator and told him the Pope had donated a sealed silver casket that contained valuable papers pertaining to St. Paul's ministry here and that the Vatican had generously donated them to St. Agatha's, with the proviso that it be displayed at the foot of the statue of St. Paul, which had impressed his Holiness so much during his first visit. Needless to say, they were delighted. Do you recall the grotto, John?" he asked.

"I believe I do, Victor – and if I remember rightly, weren't we able to access the cave from St. Agatha's catacombs?"

"You have a good memory. Yes we could, but the passageway was sealed several years ago when the grotto was given to the Wignacourt Museum to look after. Steel gates now protect the grotto from unescorted visitors and a CCTV camera was installed at my request, though I doubt anybody monitors it." Victor paused.

"So that passage no longer exists?" John asked.

"I re-opened it without anyone being aware of the fact, so that I could visit the grotto to check on the casket late at night, when everybody was in bed. I would check that the papal seal was intact and nothing had been tampered with. I did this without fail every Thursday or Friday at about 1 am. Just over ten days ago, to my total dismay, the silver chest was gone." He drew a shuddering breath.

"And, as far as you're aware, no one but yourself here in Malta, knew of the true contents?" John asked.

"His Holiness made no mention of anyone else. Of course, several people knew of the addition of the chest and the so-called documents I had implied it contained. The local English paper, *The Times of Malta* ran a story on the gift. By the way, I would like to introduce you to my niece, who is a feature columnist with the paper. Her name is Rosaria Rodenas, and she has been assigned to cover the convention you're here to attend and has asked to meet you. I mentioned we have known each other since long before she was born. I believe she could be of great help to you and, if necessary, open some otherwise closed doors."

"I'd be delighted to meet her. Who have you told about the disappearance?"

"Well, I made an unannounced visit to the grotto first thing the morning following my discovery – needless to say, I got no sleep that night. I pointed out to the guide that the chest was missing. He said he felt sure it had been there the previous day – that would be Thursday – but he couldn't be sure as he'd only had a couple of tourists all day. My guess is that it was removed either on the Wednesday or Thursday, because there had been a school group through on Tuesday. After their visit to the grotto they came here, and one of the students asked about the silver casket they had just seen at the foot of St. Paul. The guide had mentioned that it was a gift to St. Agatha's from the Pope."

"What of the CCTV camera? Were you able to view any tapes?"

"To be honest with you, there aren't any! You see, it's designed only to enable the receptionist – who, by the way, is an unpaid volunteer – to monitor the guided tours and get an estimate of the numbers about to arrive up from the grotto and into the museum. The rest of the time the gates are secure and no one can enter, other than me of course, or by using the secret tunnel."

"And how far is the theft public knowledge?"

"Out of respect for the Church and everyone concerned, the media have agreed not to report on the theft."

"Thank God for small mercies," John sighed.

Victor nodded. "True. But where do we go from here, John?"

# Chapter 7
## (Day 2: afternoon)

"Okay," John said. "Let's recap. We know the casket was in place on the Tuesday. At what time?"

"If I recall correctly, the school group came here about 2.30 in the afternoon. I can check my diary."

"So we can assume that the deed was done sometime between 2.30 pm on Tuesday and the time of your visit at 1 am, you say, on the Friday. Is that correct?" John didn't wait for a reply.

"I presume you've spoken to all the guides and the staff at the Wignacourt?"

"Yes, to everyone," Victor confirmed.

"What about your own staff here at St. Agatha's, Victor? Is there anyone here you think could possibly be involved? And another thought just crossed my mind – do you think the thief may very well not know what he or she has stolen?"

"That thought has crossed my mind several times," Victor confessed. "Articles go missing from our churches far more regularly than the public realize. Anything of any authentic origin, particularly relating to St. Paul, would be considered priceless on the black market."

Victor paused. He seemed to hesitate. "As far as my staff is concerned ... there's one possibility. I promised myself that I wouldn't mention this to anyone, but I know I can rely on your discretion and, under the circumstances, it's best you know.

"About two months ago, I was assigned a new novice to assist me with the cataloging. Brother Darren is a prospective member of our Order, who is being tried to see if he proves suitable for admission. Such novices are assigned varying jobs here at St. Agatha's and are monitored very closely before being admitted to the priesthood.

"Now, stamp collecting has been a personal hobby of mine for several years, and one of his duties was to help me catalog my collection. It was to help me evaluate if he had an inclination for the work we do here. Two weeks after he arrived, I discovered a number of very valuable stamp packages missing."

John immediately asked, "And did you confront him?"

"Well, I said nothing at the time, but decided to watch him more closely. The next day I made a big fuss about the value of a certain package and asked him to catalog the stamps and file them away. Two days later, they were missing. That's when I challenged him."

"And...?" John prompted.

"He said that they had possibly been mislaid and he would search for them. Later that day, he arrived at my desk with the missing stamps and said he had misfiled them. The only problem was, I had looked in the file in which he claimed to have 'misplaced' them only an hour earlier. I could, of course, prove nothing, so I let the matter slide. Come to think of it, he's passionate about anything to do with St. Paul. I believe he may be a member of Opus Dei. He was planning a website devoted to St. Paul's travels, particularly regarding the shipwreck that brought him here to our beloved island."

"Does that mean you suspect him?" John asked.

"No, not really. I'm actually very fond of young Darren," Victor hastened to add. "He's had a difficult childhood and seems in need of love and guidance. I shouldn't say this, but my personal opinion is that he's too unstable for our Order and would be better suited to a ... a more worldly calling."

"That might just be what he has in mind," John retorted. "I think at this point, Victor, I would like to visit the scene of the crime. I don't know what I can contribute – I know we archaeologists are sometimes referred to as historical detectives, but criminal cases are not exactly my field of expertise."

"I understand, John. Just being able to share the problem has been a relief I cannot describe. I consider you a dear friend and at this stage I am more than grateful for any help I can get. I was at my wits' end and didn't know where to turn. The grotto will be closed by now; we can enter through the tunnel if you wish. Give me a minute and I'll get the keys to the crypt," Victor said, as he moved to a small cupboard on the wall behind his desk.

As they entered the crypt leading to the catacombs, Victor opened a storage cupboard and removed two high-powered torches. "A big improvement on our old kerosene lamps! We will need these – there is no light in the tunnel."

Once in the crypt, the entrance to the public catacombs is to the right of the altar. On the walls of the crypt there still remain a good number of frescoes. Some of them date back to the twelfth century and are in the Byzantine style. The others, which are in the Greek style, date back to the fifteenth century. There are thirty images of saints, out of which thirteen represent St. Agatha. The remainder represent bishop saints, virgin and martyr saints.

The fifteenth century frescoes are attributed to the Sicilian painter Salvatore D'Antonio, John recalled. These were donated to the crypt by various devotees, offered in thanksgiving. Other paintings are still visible on the ceiling of the entrance to the right.

Victor led John to the left, where there was an entrance covered with an iron gate, securely locked. He unlocked the gate and switched on his torch. John did likewise.

The passageway through the partly restored catacombs was not easy to navigate. As John shone his torch beam from side to side, he noted the partly excavated tombs, and a flood of memories of those early days of discovery came back to him. John recalled painstakingly sifting through the rubble to rescue the skeletal remains of the original inhabitants.

Their journey took them under two main roads: Triq Hal Bajjada, where John had parked his car, and the main square in front of St. Paul's Church. Victor and his team had placed additional support beams in the area where the catacombs passed under these busy intersections.

"You've done a good job, Victor, but the beams look a little shaky. I guess the traffic wasn't a problem when the original catacombs were cut."

"I know, John. I've been meaning to do something about them; it's been some years since I put them in place. The traffic above has increased considerably since then," Victor said.

As they rounded the final corner, they came to a large boulder blocking their path.

"I can't help but think of the similarity between the discovery of our Lord's resurrection and my shock when I rolled back the stone and discovered the silver casket missing." Victor's voice became very emotional.

## In the Image of His God

"Do you need help with that?" John asked. "It looks awfully heavy."

"I've been rolling it back every Friday for the last few years," Victor remarked. "I'm sure I can manage one more time."

The lights were on in the sacred grotto. John noticed that the red light on the CCTV was not illuminated. Victor saw the direction of his gaze.

"The receptionist in the museum turns off the camera before he leaves. The lights are on an automatic timer and should go off in about another hour," Victor said, glancing at his watch.

"This," said Victor, pointing to the base of the statue of St. Paul, "is where the chest was located prior to its disappearance."

John examined the stone floor around the statue. He had no idea what he was looking for, but it seemed the natural thing to do. He found nothing.

"And you say these gates are sealed at all times when a guard isn't present?"

Victor nodded.

"I don't know, Victor. I'm as baffled as you are. I need time to process the facts and check out a few things this evening. What say we meet again tomorrow afternoon? I'll meet your niece if she's available in the morning and get together with you again at St. Agatha's tomorrow afternoon. We can take it from there."

Together they made their way back through the labyrinth of graves. As they passed through the section under the main roads, John's attention was again drawn to the inadequate support pillars. A passing truck shook a piece of the overhead rubble loose onto John's head.

"Ouch!" exclaimed John, causing Victor to turn and grin.

"Now you know what I go through nearly every day!" he joked.

# Chapter 8
(Day 2: early evening)

John called Rosaria as soon as he got back to his hotel after a brief detour to his favorite spots on the island. Her voice was pleasant and friendly. She sounded relieved that he had called and that he had also met with Victor. They agreed to a breakfast meeting at John's hotel at 9 the next morning.

John settled down at his laptop for the evening. He intended to highlight the Church's belief in the Shroud as part of his dinner presentation. Letting his mind drift, he recalled a speech made by John Paul II in 1998. He typed in the keywords and hit the search button.

***ADDRESS OF HIS HOLINESS POPE JOHN PAUL II***

***Sunday, 24 May 1998***

***Dear Brothers and Sisters,***

***1. With my gaze turned to the Shroud, I would like to extend a cordial greeting to you all, the faithful of the Church of Turin. I greet the pilgrims who have come from every part of the world at the***

*time of this public exposition to look at one of the most unsettling signs of the Redeemer's suffering love.*

*As I entered the cathedral, which still shows the scars of last year's terrible fire, I paused in adoration before the Eucharist, the sacrament which is the focus of the Church's attention and, under humble appearances, contains the true, real and substantial presence of Christ. In the light of Christ's presence in our midst, I then stopped before the Shroud, the precious Linen that can help us better to understand the mystery of the love of God's Son for us. Before the Shroud, the intense and agonizing image of an unspeakable torment, I wish to thank the Lord for this unique gift, which asks for the believer's loving attention and complete willingness to follow the Lord.*

*2. The Shroud is a challenge to our intelligence. It first of all requires of every person, particularly the researcher, that he humbly grasp the profound message it sends to his reason and his life. The mysterious fascination of the Shroud forces questions to be raised about the sacred Linen and the historical life of Jesus. Since it is not a matter of faith, the Church has no specific competence to pronounce on these questions. She entrusts to scientists the task of continuing to investigate, so that satisfactory answers may be found to the questions connected with this Sheet, which, according to tradition, wrapped the body of our Redeemer after he had been taken down from the cross. The Church urges that the Shroud be studied without pre-established positions that take for granted results that are not such; she invites them to act with interior freedom and attentive respect for both scientific methodology and the sensibilities of believers.*

*3. For the believer, what counts above all is that the Shroud is a mirror of the Gospel. In fact, if we reflect on the sacred Linen, we cannot escape the idea that the image it presents has such a profound relationship with what the Gospels tell of Jesus' passion and death, that every sensitive person feels inwardly touched and moved at beholding it. Whoever approaches it is also aware that the Shroud does not hold people's hearts to itself, but turns them to him, at whose service the Father's loving providence has put it. Therefore, it is right to foster an awareness of the precious value of this image, which everyone sees and no one at present can explain. For every thoughtful person it is a reason for deep reflection, which can even involve one's life. The Shroud is thus a truly unique sign that points to Jesus, the true Word of the Father, and invites us to pattern our lives on the life of the One who gave himself for us.*

*4. The image of human suffering is reflected in the Shroud. It reminds modern man, often distracted by prosperity and technological achievements, of the tragic situation of his many brothers and sisters, and invites him to question himself about the mystery of suffering in order to explore its causes. The imprint left by the tortured body of the Crucified One, which attests to the tremendous human capacity for causing pain and death to one's fellow man, stands as an icon of the suffering of the innocent in every age: of the countless tragedies that have marked past history and the dramas that continue to unfold in the world. Before the Shroud, how can we not think of the millions of people who die of hunger, of the horrors committed in the many wars that soak nations in blood, of the brutal exploitation of women and children, of the millions of human beings who live in hardship and humiliation on the edges of great cities, especially in developing countries? How can we not recall with dismay and pity those who do not enjoy basic civil rights, the victims of torture and terrorism, the slaves of criminal organizations? By calling to mind these tragic situations, the Shroud not only spurs us to abandon our selfishness but leads us to discover the mystery of suffering, which, sanctified by Christ's sacrifice, achieves salvation for all humanity. Death is not the ultimate goal of human existence*

*5. The Shroud is also an image of God's love as well as of human sin. It invites us to rediscover the ultimate reason for Jesus' redeeming death. In the incomparable suffering that it documents, the love of the One who "so loved the world that he gave his only Son" (Jn 3: 16) is made almost tangible and reveals its astonishing dimensions. In its presence believers can only exclaim in all truth:*

*"Lord, you could not love me more!", and immediately realize that sin is responsible for that suffering: the sins of every human being.*

*As it speaks to us of love and sin, the Shroud invites us all to impress upon our spirit the face of God's love, to remove from it the tremendous reality of sin. Contemplation of that tortured Body helps contemporary man to free himself from the superficiality of the selfishness with which he frequently treats love and sin. Echoing the word of God and centuries of Christian consciousness, the Shroud whispers: believe in God's love, the greatest treasure given to humanity, and flee from sin, the greatest misfortune in history.*

*6. The Shroud is also an image of powerlessness: the powerlessness of death, in which the ultimate consequence of the mystery of the Incarnation is revealed. The burial cloth spurs us to measure ourselves against the most troubling aspect of the mystery of the Incarnation, which is also the one that shows with how much truth God truly became man, taking on our condition in all things, except sin. Everyone is shaken by the thought that not even the Son of God withstood the power of death, but we are all moved at the thought that he so shared our human condition as willingly to subject himself to the total powerlessness of the moment when life is spent. It is the experience of Holy Saturday, an important stage on Jesus' path to Glory, from which a ray of light shines on the sorrow and death of every person. By reminding us of Christ's victory, faith gives us the certainty that the grave is not the ultimate goal of existence. God calls us to resurrection and immortal life.*

*7. The Shroud is an image of silence. There is a tragic silence of incommunicability, which finds its greatest expression in death, and there is the silence of fruitfulness, which belongs to whoever refrains from being heard outwardly in order to delve to the roots of truth and life. The Shroud expresses not only the silence of death but also the courageous and fruitful silence of triumph over the transitory, through total immersion in God's eternal present. It thus offers a moving confirmation of the fact that the merciful omnipotence of our God is not restrained by any power of evil, but knows instead how to make the very power of evil contribute to good. Our age needs to rediscover the fruitfulness of silence, in order to overcome the dissipation of sounds, images and chatter that too often prevent the voice of God from being heard.*

*8. Dear brothers and sisters: your Archbishop, dear Cardinal Giovanni Saldarini, the Pontifical Guardian of the Holy Shroud, has offered the following words as the motto of this Solemn Exposition: "All will see your salvation". Yes, the pilgrimage that great throngs are making to this city is precisely a "coming to see" this tragic and enlightening sign of the Passion, which proclaims the Redeemer's love. This icon of Christ abandoned in the dramatic and solemn state of death, which for centuries has been the subject of significant representations and for 100 years, thanks to photography, has been so frequently reproduced, urges us to go to the heart of the mystery of life and death, to discover the great and consoling message it has left us.*

*The Shroud shows us Jesus at the moment of his greatest helplessness and reminds us that in the abasement of that death lies the salvation of the whole world. The Shroud thus becomes an invitation to face every experience, including that of suffering and extreme helplessness, with the attitude of those who believe that God's merciful love overcomes every poverty, every limitation, every temptation to despair.*

*May the Spirit of God, who dwells in our hearts, instill in everyone the desire and generosity necessary for accepting the Shroud's message and for making it the decisive inspiration of our lives.*

*Anima Chrisi, sanctifica me! Corpus Christi, salva me! Passio Christi, conforta me! Intra vulnera tua, absconde me!*

John closed his laptop. Something was bothering him, though he couldn't seem to place it. Glancing at his watch, he realized he hadn't eaten yet, but he didn't feel up to going to the restaurant. He called room service to order a light meal. He had a range of options, but had to cut out the more fiery ones. His stomach wasn't as cast iron as it used to be.

As he hung up, something clicked in his brain. *Fiery! Didn't a fire damage the Shroud?* Anticipating another clue to the whole mystery, John headed back to his laptop.

# Chapter 9
(Day 2: late evening)

The Pope's speech had triggered a memory of the fire that nearly destroyed the Cathedral in Turin and the Holy Shroud with it, just one year before the Pope's historic address. He hit the search button again:

Turín FIRE 1997     April 12th, 1997

*Cardinal Saldarini said a mass of thanksgiving on Sunday, in the Sanctuary of Consolata, the most ancient in Turin. The following is the text of his official press release:*

*The fire, which broke out during the night in Chapel of Guarini, next to the Cathedral of Turin, has damaged all the structure and the ornaments of the Chapel itself, but – thanks to God – the reliquary of the Sindon has not been damaged in any way. The building of the Cathedral itself has been entirely saved from the flames, while unfortunately the most serious damage is to be found in the Chapel and in the contiguous building of the Royal Palace. Here, I wish to extend my heartfelt thanks to all those who, starting with the firemen, the civil authorities, soldiers and police, did everything in their power during this emergency. The reliquary with the Shroud, immediately removed from the Cathedral, is being kept in a safe place.*

***This serious episode has happened during the time in which our Church is preparing, in the anticipation of the Great Jubilee of the Third Millennium, for the solemn ostension of the Sindon, in the month of April 1998. The destructive fire, the very serious material damage to a monument of faith and art, represents however, for all of us Turinese – and for all the world that in these hours is looking at Turin – a test, an appeal, a Grace. A test of our faith and, also of our capacity as believers and as citizens, attached to those treasures which are at the roots of our culture and of our combined way of life. Those flames are also an appeal: a precise appeal to the responsibility which we all have, to defend and protect the religious, artistic and historic heritage so closely linked to all our experience as a Church and City. Why did it happen? In today's Gospel Jesus told us "Don't be afraid", something that He can say and that we can hear Him say to us when something terrible happens. The Cathedral, and the Sindon of which I am guardian, have been touched by disaster and saved. It is the way worthy of the measure of God when he says, "Don't be afraid". Now we are really assured that he walks on the water, climbs on our boat and leads us to the shore. In faith I give thanks for this sign.***

*+ Giovanni Card. Saldarini*
***Pontifical Custodian of the Holy Shroud***
***Turin, April 12th, 1997***

*My God*! John thought. *The perfect cover to switch the shrouds!*

There was little doubt that Pope John Paul II truly believed that the Shroud of Turin was indeed the burial cloth in which Christ was wrapped following his crucifixion. John printed a copy to use in his dinner speech. He lay back on his bed and reviewed the day's happenings. Thoughts of Opus Dei and the legendary Illuminati rushed through his head. So much had been written about and attributed to these secret societies over the last few years.

The Catholic Church had long been the suggested target of the Illuminati in their quest for world domination. The Church had a greater influence around the world than any single world power or country. Attempts to destabilize the governments of the world paled significantly compared to discrediting the Catholic Church.

The mysterious and suspicious deaths of two pontiffs had been immediately covered up.

John Paul 1, seen by many as a threat to corruption in the Vatican, called four of his cardinals together for a secret meeting in late September 1978. No one knew what was discussed. A few days later, the Pope was found dead! A Russian bishop had died mysteriously in the Pope's presence only twenty-three days earlier.

All this a few weeks before the international STURP group was due to examine the Shroud ...

John finished his soup, lost in thought. With a memory flickering in his brain, he headed back to his laptop and went to shroud.com.

***In October of 1978 the STURP team spent 120 continuous hours conducting their examination of the Shroud.***

***To this day, scientists around the world use the data gathered by STURP for their Shroud research. Even the Vatican has stated that the material gathered in 1978 constitutes the official scientific data available for Shroud research and it has no plans to allow any further testing, except in the area of conservation of the cloth itself. Although carbon dating of the Shroud in 1988 yielded a 12th century date, newly discovered information has led many researchers to believe the carbon date is in error. The controversy continues. In any case, no serious study of the Shroud of Turin can ignore the immense volume of scientific facts determined from the 1978 data, and a close look at the 1978 test results must be on the agenda of any intelligent person interested in deciding for himself.***

## In the Image of His God

John was well aware of the STURP group's findings – he knew their report almost by heart. He located it on the site and read:

## *A Summary of STURP's Conclusions*

*After years of exhaustive study and evaluation of the data, STURP issued its Final Report in 1981. The following official conclusions are reproduced verbatim from that report: Barry Schwortz*

> *No pigments, paints, dyes or stains have been found on the fibrils. X-ray, fluorescence and microchemistry on the fibrils preclude the possibility of paint being used as a method for creating the image. Ultra Violet and infrared evaluation confirm these studies. Computer image enhancement and analysis by a device known as a VP-8 image analyzer show that the image has unique, three-dimensional information encoded in it. Micro chemical evaluation has indicated no evidence of any spices, oils, or any biochemicals known to be produced by the body in life or in death. It is clear that there has been a direct contact of the Shroud with a body, which explains certain features such as scourge marks, as well as the blood. However, while this type of contact might explain some of the features of the torso, it is totally incapable of explaining the image of the face with the high resolution that has been amply demonstrated by photography. The basic problem from a scientific point of view is that some explanations, which might be tenable from a chemical point of view, are precluded by physics. Contrariwise, certain physical explanations, which may be attractive, are completely precluded by the chemistry. For an adequate explanation for the image of the Shroud, one must have an explanation which is scientifically sound, from a physical, chemical, biological and medical viewpoint. At the present, this type of solu-*

*tion does not appear to be obtainable by the best efforts of the members of the Shroud Team. Furthermore, experiments in physics and chemistry with old linen have failed to reproduce adequately the phenomenon presented by the Shroud of Turin. The scientific consensus is that the image was produced by something which resulted in oxidation, dehydration and conjugation of the polysaccharide structure of the micro fibrils of the linen itself. Such changes can be duplicated in the laboratory by certain chemical and physical processes. A similar type of change in linen can be obtained by sulfuric acid or heat. However, there are no chemical or physical methods known which can account for the totality of the image, nor can any combination of physical, chemical, biological or medical circumstances explain the image adequately.*

*Thus, the answer to the question of how the image was produced or what produced the image remains, now, as it has in the past, a mystery.*

*We can conclude for now that the Shroud image is that of a real human form of a scourged, crucified man. It is not the product of an artist. The bloodstains are composed of hemoglobin and also give a positive test for serum albumin. The image is an ongoing mystery and until further chemical studies are made, perhaps by this group of scientists, or perhaps by some scientists in the future, the problem remains unsolved.*

As John headed for bed, he recalled that in the same month following the testing, on 16 October 1978, Karol Wojtyla was elected Pope, becoming the Catholic Church's first non-Italian pontiff in over 450 years, and history's first Slavic pope. He took the name John Paul II as a tribute to his predecessor, John Paul I, whose term lasted just over one month.

Suddenly John had a feeling that there was something far more sinister than just the theft of a missing artifact at play here. What exactly had he gotten himself into? On that thought, he closed his eyes and, worn out by information overload, drifted into an uneasy sleep.

# Chapter 10
(Day 3: morning)

Rosaria arrived at John's hotel promptly at 9 am. As she walked into the restaurant, John was struck by her confidence, her grace and her loveliness. Her deep brown eyes sparkled with vivacity. The silky brown hair brushing her shoulders framed a lovely face and her petite figure left no doubt about her gender!

She held out her hand. "Good morning, Dr. Peters."

He looked into her deep brown eyes.

"Hello, Rosaria. And what's all this 'Dr. Peters' formality? Call me John, please."

"Okay, John." Her smile extended to her eyes. "Victor has told me so much about you. I've really been looking forward to this meeting."

It was a beautiful morning and they enjoyed their breakfast on the terrace overlooking the calm waters of the Mediterranean. John, on the other hand, was far from calm. His deepening concern that there was much more involved here than a missing relic had been eating at him all night.

Rosaria was delightful. They hit it off together immediately. She was obviously deeply worried about Victor and felt helpless about the predicament he now found himself in.

John, at the very least, was another mind to help tackle the problem before them. She told him all she knew and had deduced since the incident. It was not a lot. And, of course, she had no clue about the real contents of the missing casket.

John suggested they move to his room, where they would be assured of reasonable privacy.

"How do you want to do this?" he asked. "I understand you are writing a piece on the convention. Perhaps we should get that out of the way first?"

"Thank you, that sounds like a good idea. Perhaps you'd like to start by telling me how you got involved with the Shroud. I have the press release on the theme of the convention and the goals of the Shroud Society. I'd like to give the story a personal touch as you have a background here, even if it was some time ago," she said, quickly adding, "Please forgive me, I didn't mean that to sound rude!"

"Not at all. Fifty years is a fair time to be absent from somewhere that meant so much to me."

Rosaria clicked on a tiny recorder and placed it on the table between them. "Do you mind, John? It's just so I don't miss anything." He nodded.

"Of course, I had no idea of the Shroud's existence when I was here – it was some considerable years after I got involved in broadcasting that the mystery of the image on the cloth was brought to my attention by one of my listeners."

"I know of your interviews," she said. "How did that come about?"

"Some time later, following the 1978 testing of the Shroud by the STURP group, my producer suggested we do a follow-up on our original story and we invited the members of the STURP group to take part in a series of live interviews on their findings. They were, of course, scattered around the globe. I was in Australia at the time. I was able to contact seven of the most influential experts, including some of the original team."

"Would you happen to have their names and affiliations?" Rosaria asked. "That would provide good background for my story."

"I can certainly help you there," John smiled. "Of course, the organizations are ones they were affiliated with back in 1978. The experts I met were: Al Adler of Western Connecticut State University; Barrie M. Schwortz of Barrie Schwortz Studios; Vernon D. Miller of Brooks Institute of Photography; John Heller of the New England Institute; Father Rinaldi, who was Keeper of the Shroud at Turin Cathedral; Walter McCrone of the McCrone Research Institute; and Ian Wilson, who is the noted author of several books on the Shroud.

"The McCrone Research Institute," he added, "was founded by Walter McCrone, who was a noted microscopist, and was active in Shroud research for many years."

"And who," Rosaria asked, "were the others involved?"

John reached for his briefcase and removed a plastic folder from which he handed her a list of the STURP team he had obtained from shroud.com.

**Investigators for the Shroud of Turin Research Project (STURP) include:**

*Joseph S. Accetta, Lockheed Corporation\**

*Steven Baumgart, U.S. Air Force Weapons Laboratories\**

*John D. German, U.S. Air Force Weapons Laboratories\**

# In the Image of His God

*Ernest H. Brooks II, Brooks Institute of Photography\**

*Mark Evans, Brooks Institute of Photography\**

*Vernon D. Miller, Brooks Institute of Photography\**

*Robert Bucklin, Harris County, Texas, Medical Examiner's Office*

*Donald Devan, Oceanographic Services Inc.\**

*Rudolph J. Dichtl, University of Colorado\**

*Robert Dinegar, Los Alamos National Scientific Laboratories\**

*Donald & Joan Janney, Los Alamos National Scientific Laboratories\**

*J. Ronald London, Los Alamos National Scientific Laboratories\**

*Roger A. Morris, Los Alamos National Scientific Laboratories\**

*Ray Rogers, Los Alamos National Scientific Laboratories\**

*Larry Schwalbe, Los Alamos National Scientific Laboratories*

*Diane Soran, Los Alamos National Scientific Laboratories*

*Kenneth E. Stevenson, IBM\**

*Al Adler, Western Connecticut State University*

*Thomas F. D'Muhala, Nuclear Technology Corporation\**

*Jim Drusik, Los Angeles County Museum*

*Joseph Gambescia, St. Agnes Medical Center*

*Roger & Marty Gilbert, Oriel Corporation\**

*Thomas Haverty, Rocky Mountain Thermograph\**

*John Heller, New England Institute*

*John P. Jackson, U.S. Air Force Academy\**

*Eric J. Jumper, U.S. Air Force Academy\**

*Jean Lorre, Jet Propulsion Laboratory\**

*Donald J. Lynn, Jet Propulsion Laboratory\**

*Robert W. Mottern, Sandia Laboratories\**

*Samuel Pellicori, Santa Barbara Research Center\**

*Note: The researchers marked with an \* participated directly in the 1978 Examination in Turin. All others are STURP research members who worked with the data or samples after the team returned to the United States.*

"There is no doubt about the legitimacy of such an honor roll of scientific minds," John pointed out. "If you like, I'll play you the interviews. I think you'll be amazed at the positive findings of the group."

"Do you have a spare set of CDs? I could listen to them at home this evening. That way we'll have more time to discuss what you can tell me about the Shroud."

"Of course," John agreed. "That makes better sense. Do carry on with your questions."

"Are you a religious man, John? What did *you* make of the Shroud?"

Her question caught John off guard. "I guess, like most of us, I have my own personal beliefs ... I was a member of the Mormon Church for many years. There is no doubt that the STURP interviews left me with a very real sense of the pain and suffering that Christ must have endured ... yes, it is fair to say it strengthened my belief. From that time until the carbon dating in 1988, I firmly believed it to be a first-century cloth."

"What can you tell me about the history of the Shroud itself?" she asked.

"I have a printed history of the Shroud that I'd be happy to share with you, but here, in a nutshell, is what we know of its travels," John said, settling back in his story-telling mode.

"By the way, all this information is available on Barrie Schwortz's great website, shroud.com. We've been good friends since the Shroud interviews and I know he won't mind you quoting from the site. I'm sure that he'd appreciate the courtesy of letting him know what you do use in your article. Of course, a reference to his site would be appreciated as well. I'm sure I don't have to tell you anything about journalistic protocol."

Rosaria nodded. "Any other source you recommend?"

"I also interviewed the author Ian Wilson. His 1998 book, *The Blood and the Shroud*, which includes the earlier, more speculative and 'circumstantial' material as well, suggests that the history of the Shroud of Turin can be best studied by dividing it into two specific categories. The general consensus of even the most skeptical researchers is to accept 1350 A.D. as the beginning of the undisputed or documented history of the Shroud of Turin."

"Is that because of the carbon dating verification?"

"Yes," John concurred. "That is the approximate date determined by the 1988 carbon dating of the cloth."

Settling back in his chair, he continued his narration. "Although there is a significant amount of evidence supporting the Shroud's existence prior to the mid-1300s, much of it is, in fact, circumstantial and remains mostly unproven. This, coupled with the fact that many – including a major scientific authority – believe the carbon dating process has a much larger margin of inaccuracy than originally thought, has supported the 'Leonardo da Vinci theory' which I will explain to you later.

"The first of the Christian Orders contained in the Chivalric system relates the story of St. Paul's arrival in Malta."

Rosaria reluctantly interrupted, "Sorry to break in, John, and please excuse my ignorance. What is the 'Chivalric system'?"

John felt a prickle of irritation, but as he looked at her puzzled face he realized she was drinking in every word.

"To describe it simply, the belief of the Knights Templar. The belief in the Holy Trinity."

"Thanks," she said. "Please go on."

"In the next portion of the order the history of the Knights of Malta is explained and two theories have come forward that relate to the Templars having been involved with the Shroud; one which supports the fact that it is the burial cloth of Christ and the other which, of course, refutes it.

"It was in 1204 that the Knights Templar crusaders ransacked the city of Constantinople. Many believe it was at that time they took the Shroud. Author Ian Wilson whom, as I told you, I interviewed and who also wrote the book *The Shroud of Turin: Burial Cloth Of Jesus?* claims that the head that the Templars were accused of worshipping –referred to as the 'Mandylion' – was, in fact, the image of Christ on the Shroud. He believes that the Shroud, when folded, shows just the head and was referred to as the 'Mandylion'."

"You mean the head the Templars venerated was actually the image of Christ?" Rosaria asked.

"Yes," John replied, "according to Ian. However, the authors Christopher Knight and Robert Lomas in their two books, *The Hiram Key* and *The Second Messiah*, have a totally different Mandylion theory. They believe that the image referred to as the Mandylion and the one on the Shroud is actually Jacques de Molay, said to be the last Grand Master of the Knights Templar, who was tortured in a similar fashion to Christ some months before his execution in 1307."

"Could that be true?" Rosaria broke in. "On what is such a claim based?"

"The resemblance to Christ," John said. "However, the description of De Molay's six-foot frame as found in medieval woodcuts – shoulder-length hair parted in the center, a long nose and a full beard – have caused many to argue that this could not be the case. You see, De Molay's hair would have been cut, as it was forbidden for Templars to have long hair. As he spent his last seven years in prison, it is unlikely he would have enjoyed the opportunity for a hair cut! In their book the authors put forward a number of possibilities for the formation of the image, none of which hold much water in the light of more recent scientific findings on the image on the Shroud," John concluded.

"So these authors were mistaken?"

"Whether you believe Ian Wilson or the findings of Knight and Lomas, there is little doubt the Templars were involved in the history of the Shroud. Lynn Picknet and Clive Prince published a different theory in their work *Turin Shroud: In Whose Image?* The duo claims that Leonardo da Vinci created an early photographic technique and is responsible for the image on the Shroud of Turin."

"Is that the Da Vinci theory you were talking about?" Rosaria asked, leaning forward, her face alight with interest.

"In a nutshell, yes," John replied, smiling. "Getting back to the Knights Templar," he continued, "they were formed in 1119, and became one of the most powerful Christian groups in the area. They proved outstanding warriors and their soldiers wore a black surcoat with a white cross on the front. They were still a religious order and as such received untold privileges, answering only to the Pope himself. At one time they were said to have over 140 estates and many great forts in the Holy Land. The Holy Roman Emperor is said to have pledged his protection to the Templars in the year 1185.

"Their colorful history continued throughout the ensuing seven years and the Knights moved around the Mediterranean, eventually settling in Malta in 1530. They were required to pay an annual fee of a single Maltese Falcon to the King of Spain's representative. I'm sure you've heard the story many times." John laughed.

Rosaria smiled back. "Not really. This is all most interesting. And how is it connected to the Shroud?"

"Well, getting back to that, the Shroud really came to light around 1349. A French knight named Geoffrey de Charnay is believed to have acquired the Shroud in Constantinople. It is recorded that he put the Shroud on display to commemorate his miraculous escape from the British. Large crowds are reported to have visited his chapel at Lirey, France, in 1355. A Bishop Henri apparently disbelieved in the authenticity of the Shroud and ordered the exposition closed."

"So what happened to the Shroud?" Rosaria asked.

"The Shroud was secreted away for safekeeping. The following year, Geoffrey de Charnay was killed, but the Shroud remained in his family's possession. In fact," he added grimly, "the Shroud has been linked to a large number of mysterious deaths, that I'll tell you about later."

He watched Rosaria absorb the information, gratified by her sincere interest.

"We next hear of the Shroud in 1389, when the King of France, Charles VI, ordered the Shroud seized. However, the bailiffs at Troyes, where the Shroud was kept, sealed the doors, preventing its removal. The King's First Sergeant reported to the bailiffs of Troyes that he had informed the dean and canons of the Lirey Church that – and I quote here – 'the cloth has now verbally been put into the hands of our lord the king. The decision has also been conveyed to a squire of the de Charnay household for conveyance to his master'.

"The then bishop, Pierre d'Arcis of Troyes, apparently appealed to Clement VII, the antipope, and the 'executioner of Cesena', as he became known –"

"What," Rosaria broke in, "or should I ask who, is an antipope?"

"A person who makes a widely accepted claim to be the lawful Pope, in opposition to the Pope recognized by the Roman Catholic Church," John explained.

"And why the 'executioner' tag?"

"Well, he reportedly authorized the massacre of over 4,000 persons to quell a rebellion in the Pontifical States," John explained.

"The Bishop," he continued, "claimed that the cloth was a clever forgery and that it was being claimed as the true Shroud in which Jesus's body was wrapped only to attract crowds of pilgrims. Clement VII told the Bishop to shut up and informed the de Charnay family that they could continue with the exhibit."

Rosaria frowned. "So there were doubts about the authenticity of the Shroud back then?"

"Apparently, but the Bishop wasn't believed. In 1418, the Shroud was put on display at the Pre'du Seigneur, in a meadow on the banks of the river Doubs. Nearly fifty years later, one of the few surviving documents reported that the Shroud was in the possession of the Savoy family, transferred to Duke Louis by Margaret de Charnay. In 1465, the Duke died at Lyon and history has recorded that the acquisition of the Shroud was his greatest achievement."

John wondered if he was giving Rosaria too much information for her to follow. "Am I losing you, or do you want to hear more?"

"Oh no!" Rosaria said emphatically. "I find the whole story fascinating. I can't believe I hadn't heard of the Shroud before your intended visit."

"Well, just speak up if you've heard enough. As I said, you'll find the full story at shroud.com or I can highly recommend Ian Wilson's book *The Blood and the Shroud*, if you want all the sordid details."

"Shroud.com certainly sounds like it's worth a visit. Do you think I could take a quick look at it now, and check it out later?"

"Be my guest," John gestured to his laptop.

After five minutes of browsing, Rosaria returned to her chair. "Wow! It certainly seems exhaustive. Definitely worth many more visits. Sorry for the disruption. Please do go on."

"No problem," John said. "So where were we?"

"You'd got to the point of Duke Louis's death," Rosaria reminded him.

John continued. "Ah, yes. After the Duke's death his son, Duke Amadeus IX, was devoted to the Shroud and is said to have founded the cult of the Shroud. In 1471, the Shroud is recorded to have been transferred from Chambéry to Vercelli. A year later, Amadeus died. The following year, the Shroud was transferred again – this time to its eventual home in Turin.

"On Good Friday, in 1478, the Shroud was again exhibited, this time at Pinerolo. Soon after, Leonardo da Vinci left Florence to serve as court painter and military engineer at the court of Ludovico Sforza, Duke of Milan, known as *Il Moro*. He stayed for eighteen years. Around this time, Jean Renguis and Georges Carrelet, respectively chaplain and sacristan of the Sainte Chapelle at Chambéry, described the Shroud as 'enveloped in a red silk drape, and kept in a case covered with crimson velours, decorated with silver-gilt nails, and locked with a golden key'.

"The Savoy family would always carry the Shroud with them on their many journeys. In 1494, Leonardo began his painting of the Last Supper in Milan."

"That took him some time, didn't it?"

"You could say that," John answered. "It supposedly took him two years!"

"So that would be 1496? And what was happening to the Shroud then?"

"In 1498," John said, "if I remember correctly, there was another graphic description of the Shroud when King Louis remodeled the Sainte Chapelle in Paris. An inventory at that time details the Shroud as – and I quote again – 'a coffer covered with crimson velours, with silver gilt roses, and the sides silver and the Holy Shroud inside wrapped in a cloth of red silk'.

"Four years later, the Shroud was finally given a home in the Royal Chapel of Chambéry Castle, no longer traveling with the Savoys."

John paused for a drink of water. "In his book," he continued, "Ian says that, along with the local clergy, the Royals were present at what was called 'the ceremony of translation'. During this ceremony the Bishop of Grenoble, Laurent Alamand, formally bore the Shroud, which was in a gilt silver case, from Chambéry's Franciscan church to the Chambéry chapel. The Shroud was exhibited on the chapel's high altar, before being entrusted to the care of Archdeacon Jacques Veyron and the canons of the chapel. They put it back in its case and deposited the holy relic behind the high altar, in a hollow that had been specially made for it. It was safeguarded by an iron grill with four locks, each of which could only be opened by separate keys. Two of these keys were held by the Duke. Pope Sixtus IV named the Chambéry chapel La Sainte Chapelle."

"That's in 1502, right?"

"That's right. In 1503, following a procession including the Duke and Duchess of Savoy and three bishops, the Shroud was taken to the Monsignor's chapel. Savoy courtier Antoine de Lalaing records that 'the Shroud's authenticity has been confirmed by its having been tried by fire, boiled in oil, laundered many times, but it was not possible to efface or remove the imprint and image.'"

"It's amazing that such a detailed history exists if the cloth were not for real," Rosaria interrupted. "You mentioned several deaths in connection with the Shroud. Were these largely due to natural causes?" she asked.

"By my count, there have been over twenty-three recorded deaths of people closely associated with the Shroud. At least half of them were 'unexplained', if that's the right term," John replied.

He rose and headed for the phone. "Tell you what. Why don't I order us some coffee and then I'll bring you up to date with the final years leading up to today. Meanwhile, I'll make a printout of some information you could use."

"Good idea," Rosaria said, clicking off the recorder and replacing it in her bag.

# Chapter 11
## (Day 3: early afternoon)

John handed Rosaria a printed history of the Shroud taken from shroud.com's extracts from Ian Wilson's book.

He pointed to the year 1513. "You can follow its history from there – if you need any clarification just call me," he said.

Rosaria glanced at the sheets he had given her. "I'll do a quick read now, if that's alright with you," she said.

"Sure," John said. "I'll be working on my closing speech for the convention. If you need any questions answered, just ask."

Rosaria settled herself comfortably and looked through the pages. With growing interest, she began to read:

- *<u>1513</u>: Death at Chambéry of Marguerite's mother-in-law dowager duchess Claude. She is buried behind the high altar of the Sainte Chapelle, Chambéry, immediately facing the repository containing the Shroud.*

- **1516:** King Francis I of France journeys from Lyon to Chambéry to venerate the Shroud after his victory at Marignan. Copy of Shroud preserved in the Church of St. Gommaire at Lierre is dated to this year.

- **1530:** Death of Marguerite of Austria.

- **December 4, 1532:** Fire breaks out in the Sainte Chapelle, Chambéry, seriously damaging all its furnishings and fittings. Because the Shroud is protected by four locks, Canon Philibert Lambert and two Franciscans summon the help of a blacksmith to prise open the grille. By the time they succeed, Marguerite of Austria's Shroud casket/reliquary, as made to her orders by Lievin van Latham, has melted beyond repair by the heat. But the Shroud folded inside is preserved bar being scorched and holed by a drop of molten silver that fell on one corner.

- **April 16, 1534:** Chambéry's Poor Clare nuns repair the Shroud, sewing it onto a backing cloth (the Holland cloth), and sewing patches over the unsightliest of the damage. These repairs are completed on 2 May. Covered in cloth of gold, the Shroud is returned to the Savoy's castle in Chambéry.

- **May 4, 1647:** At a public showing this year, held in the Cathedral, some of the enormous crowd died of suffocation.

- **May 16 and 17, 1663:** Exposition of the Shroud in the Cathedral of Turin is delayed from the normal May 4 date to coincide with the wedding of Duke Carlo Emanuele II of Savoy with Francesca d'Orleans. The copy of the Shroud pre-

*served in St. Paul's Church, Rabat, Malta, was placed in contact with the Shroud at this time.*

- *<u>June 1st, 1694:</u> The Shroud is brought solemnly into the Guarini Chapel where it remained almost uninterruptedly for over three centuries.*

- *<u>November 13, 1804:</u> Private showing of the Shroud for the visit to Turin of Pope Pius VII, virtually a prisoner en route from Rome to Paris to crown Napoleon, who would be crowned by none other than the Pope. According to Sanna Solaro, 'The Pope knelt down to venerate it, then examined it in every part, kissing it with tender devotion'. Seven cardinals, eight bishops and many other notables were present.*

- *<u>May 20, 1814:</u> Solemn showing of the Shroud to mark the return of the monarchy, in the person of King Victor Emanuel. This is the first full public showing of the Shroud since 1775.*

- *<u>May 21, 1815:</u> Pope Pius VII's second presiding over an exposition of the Shroud, this time marking his return to Italy after Napoleon's defeat. He personally displays it from the balcony of the Palazzo Madama. On the Shroud being returned to its casket, the latter is sealed with the papal and royal seals.*

- *<u>May 28, 1898:</u> Public exhibition. Secondo Pia, an Italian amateur photographer, makes the first photograph of the Shroud of Turin. It ushers in a new era in the Shroud's history, the era of science.*

- *<u>April 21, 1902:</u> (Monday afternoon) Agnostic anatomy professor Yves Delage presents a paper* *on the Shroud to the Academy of Sciences, Paris, arguing for the Shroud's medical and general scientific convincingness, and stating his opinion that it genuinely wrapped the body of Christ.*

- *April 23, 1902: Paris edition of New York Herald carries headline, 'Photographs of Christ's Body found by science'.*

- *1918: Alarmed by the danger of air raids from the World War then raging, King Victor Emanuel III orders the Shroud to be put in a place of safety, on condition that it does not leave the Royal Palace. A secret underground chamber is specially constructed two floors below ground level in the southeast side of Turin's Royal Palace, with not even the contractors told its purpose. On the floor of this chamber is set a large strongbox with a complex combination lock. On 6 May, the casket of the Shroud is removed from the Royal Chapel (in which it has lain undisturbed since 1898). It is wrapped in a thick blanket of asbestos, put in a chest made of tin plate, hermetically sealed with cold solder, then carried down to the secret chamber, where it is solemnly locked inside the strongbox. Prayers are recited, after which the chamber's heavy entrance doors are locked.*

- *May 3-24, 1931: Eighth public exhibition on the occasion of the marriage of Prince Umberto of Piedmont, later to become Umberto II of Savoy, to Princes Maria Jos of Belgium. Cardinal Fossati officiates. Two million visitors flock to Turin for this occasion.*

- *May 23, 1931: Giuseppe Enrie photographs the Shroud, confirming Secondo Pia's findings. He takes three pictures of the Shroud face, one life-size; also a detail of the shoulders and back, and a seven-fold enlargement of the wound in the wrist. The photography takes place in the presence of the now seventy-six-year-old Secondo Pia and scientists of the French Academy.*

*In this same year and the following one, Dr. Pierre Barbet conducts experiments on cadavers to reconstruct the Passion of Jesus as exhibited in the Shroud's bloodstains and wound marks.*

- <u>September 24 to October 15, 1933:</u> *At the request of Pope Pius XI, the Shroud is exhibited as part of the celebrations for Holy Year. The young Silesian priest Fr. Peter Rinaldi, fluent in French and English, as well as Italian, acts as interpreter. On the final day, 15 October, the Shroud is held out in daylight on the steps of the cathedral where Dr. Pierre Barbet views it from a distance of less than a yard. He writes: 'I saw that all the images of the wounds were of a color quite different from that of the rest of the body, and this color was that of dried blood which had sunk into the stuff. There was, thus, more than the brown stains on the Shroud reproducing the outline of the corpse. The blood itself had colored the stuff by direct contact. It is difficult for one unversed in painting to define the exact color, but the foundation was red ('mauve carmine' said M. Vignon, who had a fine sense of color), diluted more or less according to the wounds'.*

- <u>September 1939:</u> *The outbreak of World War II brings European Shroud research to a halt. The Shroud is secretly taken for safety to the Benedictine Abbey of Montevergine, in the province of Avellino, northeast of Naples. There are brief stops in Rome and Naples on its journey.*

- *September 25, 1939:* *The Shroud arrives at the Abbey. Only the Prior, the Vicar-General and two of the monks are entrusted with the knowledge of what they are protecting.*

*The Shroud returns to Turin and its traditional housing in the Royal Chapel. However, with the fall of the monarchy, and because the Chapel is part of the now state-owned Royal Palace, the Shroud is technically on Italian state territory.*

- *Holy Week, 1954:* *British war hero, Group Captain Leonard Cheshire, VC, having become inspired by the Shroud face while recuperating from tuberculosis, uses touring bus to tour Britain with an exhibition of Shroud photographs.*

- *Easter, 1955:* *Group Captain Cheshire publishes articles on the Shroud in the British Picture Post and Daily Sketch.*

- *May 11, 1955:* *Cheshire receives letter from Mrs. Veronica Woollam of Gloucester, asking if her ten-year-old daughter Josephine, crippled with osteomyelitis in the hip and leg, 'could be blessed with the relic of the Holy Shroud'. Unable to travel by air because of his lungs, Cheshire takes Josephine and her mother by train, first to Portugal, for ex-King Umberto's permission, then to Turin, in the hope of her being healed via the Shroud. The Shroud is taken out of its casket, its seals are broken and Josephine is allowed to put her hand in beneath the silk covering. But it is not unrolled. Although there was no immediate change in Josephine's condition, she later recovers to lead a normal life, though she will die young.*

- *<u>June 16-18 1969</u>: On the orders of Turin's Cardinal Michele Pellegrino, the Shroud is secretly taken out of its casket for its state of preservation to be studied by a team of experts. These examine, photograph and discuss for three days, but do no direct testing. During this same period, and with the Shroud hung vertically for the purpose, Giovanni Battista Judica-Cordiglia takes the first ever Shroud photo in color, also fresh black and white ones, and ones by Woods light.*

Satisfied with his speech, John looked up to see Rosaria still skimming through the pages.

"You can read it later, if you prefer…" he suggested.

"I know, and I probably will go through it again. I might even do a whole series of articles on the Shroud, if the paper goes for the idea. If you don't mind, though, I'll just go through the rest now. I know you'll be able to explain anything I don't understand."

John walked over to Rosaria and looked over her shoulder as she continued going through each page. He pointed to the entry dated October 1972.

- *<u>October 1, 1972</u>: Attempt to set fire to the Shroud on the part of an unknown individual who breaks into the Royal Chapel after climbing over the Palace roof. The Shroud survives due to its asbestos protection within the altar shrine.*

"The Church has been increasingly concerned at the safety of the Shroud. The next public showing is not scheduled until 2025."

As Rosaria read the report of the arson attempt, she said, "I can't believe the incredible record that has been kept of the Shroud over all these years!" Her sleek head bent over the pages again, as she continued reading:

- *November 22, 1973: (Thursday) The Shroud is displayed in the Hall of the Swiss, within Turin's Royal Palace, in preparation for its first ever television showing. International journalists and some serious researchers on the subject, including Britain's Dr. David Willis and Fr. Maurus Green, are allowed to view the Shroud directly during this time.*

- *November 23, 1973: (9.15-9.45 p.m.). Pope Paul VI exhibits the Shroud for the first time ever on television, in color, and with a filmed introduction.*

- *November 24, 1973: The Shroud is secretly examined by a new Commission of experts, brought together by Cardinal Pellegrino. On this occasion Professor Gilbert Raes takes from one edge of the Shroud's frontal end one 40x13-mm sample, also from the side-strip one 40x10-mm portion, together with one 13-mm warp thread and one 12-mm weft thread. Dr. Max Frei, Swiss criminologist, is among the other specialists present, and is allowed to take 12 samples of surface dust from the Shroud's extreme frontal end, using adhesive tape to remove these. The Shroud is returned to its casket the same evening.*

- *February 19, 1976: In the U.S.A., at Sandia Laboratories, Dr. John Jackson and Bill Mottern view for the first time the Shroud's three-dimensional image via a VP8 Image Analyzer. It is a moment that would prove to be significant in Shroud history, since it catalyzed the interest of a diverse group of scientists that eventually would become the Shroud of Turin Research Project (STURP). They ultimately would spend 120 hours performing the first in-depth scientific examination of the Shroud.*

- *<u>April 1976:</u> Release of Report of the Turin Scientific Commission, with the first public information of the pollen findings of Dr. Max Frei, who claims that the Shroud's dust includes pollens from some plants that are exclusive to Israel and to Turkey, suggesting that the Shroud must at one time have been exposed to the air in these countries.*

- *<u>March 23-24, 1977:</u> First U.S. Conference of Research on the Shroud, at the Ramada Inn, Albuquerque, New Mexico, attended by Frs. Rinaldi and Otterbein, Rev. David Sox, Dr. John Robinson, filmmaker David Rolfe and many members of what would become the STURP team.*

- *<u>May 1977:</u> First experimental use, at Rochester University, New York State, U.S.A., of the accelerator mass spectrometry (AMS) method of radiocarbon dating, by which very much smaller samples can be dated than had previously been thought possible. This is the method that will be used to date the Shroud. One of the leading pioneers of this method is Rochester University's Professor Harry Gove.*

- *<u>June 24, 1977:</u> Rev. David Sox, General Secre-*

*tary of the newly formed British Society for the Turin Shroud, writes to Professor Harry Gove of Rochester, following an article in Time magazine about the new radiocarbon dating technique.*

- *September 16-17, 1977: A Symposium on the Shroud held at the Anglican Institute of Christian Studies, London, with Drs. Jackson, Jumper, Frei, and McCrone among the speakers, also Frs. Rinaldi and Otterbein, Monsignor Ricci, and Don Coero-Borga.*

- *August 6, 1978: Sudden death of Pope Paul VI, who had expected to visit Turin to view the Shroud during the period of the expositions, one of his only two out-of-Rome engagements penciled in for the autumn. Convening of conclave to elect the next Pope.*

- *August 26, 1978: The Shroud is exhibited at inaugural Mass on the first day of a five-week-long period of expositions commemorating the 400th anniversary of the Shroud in Turin. It is the first public exhibition since 1933. In the very same hour of the inaugural Mass, Cardinal Luciani of Venice is proclaimed Pope in Rome, becoming Pope John Paul I, to live just thirty-three days more. During the five weeks the Shroud is publicly displayed, more than 3.5 million visitors view the cloth.*

- *September 1, 1978: Among the pilgrims who view the Shroud on this day is Cardinal Karol Wojtyla of Poland, shortly to become Pope John Paul II.*

- *September 2-3, 1978: In Amston, Connecticut, Dr. John Jackson's group of scientists, at this* time calling themselves the United States Conference of Research on the Shroud of Turin, meet to finalize their plans, following Turin having agreed to a twenty-four-hour test period on 9 October. This meeting would become known as the 'Dry Run' and was the first time that the entire team assembled together. They spend their time reviewing the planned experiments and testing their equipment, including the special table designed to hold the Shroud. They also sign the agreement that formally creates the Shroud of Turin Research Project (STURP).

- *September 28, 1978: Sudden death of Pope John Paul I. While Cardinal of Venice, he had planned to visit the Shroud on 21 September and was rumored to have been intending a quiet private visit before the close of the exposition.*

- *September 29, 1978: The STURP team departs the United States for Turin under a cloud of doubt, concerned that the death of Pope John Paul I the night before might cause the cancellation of their testing.*

- *October 5, 1978: At 2:30 p.m., the truck bearing eighty cases of delicate STURP equipment finally enters the courtyard of the Royal Palace. The team begins the task of unloading the truck and moving the crates of instruments into the Hall of Visiting Princes. They are five days behind schedule.*

- *October 8, 1978: At around 10:45 p.m., and slightly ahead of schedule, the Shroud is removed from public display and taken through the Guarini Chapel into the Hall of Visiting Princes within Turin's Royal Palace. Thus begins a five-*

*day period of examination, photography and sample taking by STURP. John Jackson's group of scientists from the U.S.A., Dr. Max Frei, Giovanni Riggi, Professor Pierluigi Baima-Bollone and others carry out independent research programs alongside. During this time, the Shroud is lengthily submitted to photographic floodlighting, to low-power X-rays and to narrow band ultraviolet light. Dozens of pieces of sticky tape are pressed onto its surface and removed. A side edge is unstitched and an apparatus inserted between the Shroud and its backing cloth to examine the underside, which has not been seen in over 400 years. The bottom edge (at the foot of the frontal image) is also unstitched and examined. On the night of 9 October Baima Bollone obtains sample of Shroud bloodstain by mechanically disentangling warp and weft threads in the area of the 'small of the back' bloodstain on the Shroud's dorsal image.*

- <u>*October 8-12, 1978:*</u> *STURP continues its around-the-clock examination of the Shroud, performing dozens of tests, taking thousands of photographs, photomicrographs, x-rays and spectra. A total of 120 continuous hours of testing is done, with team members working on different parts of the Shroud simultaneously. This is the most in-depth series of tests ever performed on the Shroud of Turin.*

- <u>*October 13, 1978:*</u> *(Friday) STURP completes their scientific work during the evening of this day. The Shroud is returned to its casket the following morning.*

*En route back to New Mexico, Dr. Ray Rogers stops off in Chicago and hand-delivers to Dr.*

*Walter McCrone's laboratory thirty-two of the sticky tape samples taken from the Shroud.*

- *December 25, 1978: Dr. Walter McCrone begins examination of image samples from the Shroud.*

- *March 24-25, 1979: STURP holds its 'First Data Analysis Workshop' on the Shroud, in Santa Barbara, California. According to their preliminary findings, the image shows no evidence of the hand of an artist; the body image does not appear to be any form of scorch; and the blood image was probably present before the body image. But Walter McCrone claims he has found evidence of an artist and stuns the meeting by stating, 'anybody who is emotionally wrapped up in the Shroud should start to consider the possibility that he better relax his emotions'. McCrone's views are not shared by STURP. Thus begins a highly polarized, long-term, often adversarial relationship between McCrone and STURP.*

- *April 13, 1980: On a visit to Turin, Pope John Paul II has a private showing of the Shroud and kisses the cloth's hem.*

- *May 13, 1981: (Wednesday) Dr. John Jackson, Fr. Adam Otterbein and other STURP representatives are in St. Peter's Square awaiting an audience with Pope John Paul II to report to him on the 1978 testing when the Pope is shot by Turkish gunman Mehmet Ali Agca.*

- *December 1981: STURP informs the Turin authorities that the Arizona, Brookhaven, Oxford and Rochester laboratories have all agreed to participate in a radiocarbon- dating of the Shroud.*

- *January 14, 1983:* Death of Dr. Max Frei, leaving unfinished the book he was writing on his pollen findings. His estate, with all his Shroud materials, passes to his widow Gertrud and their son Ulrich.

- *March 18, 1983:* Death of ex-king Umberto II in Cascais. The Shroud's formal owner, his will discloses that he has bequeathed the Shroud to the Pope and his successors, with the proviso that the cloth stays in Turin.

- *February 15, 1985:* Jesuit priest Father Francis Filas, best known for his controversial discovery of inscriptions on the coins in the eyes of the man of the Shroud, dies of a heart attack in his residence at Loyola University, Chicago, at the age of 69. His claims that the inscriptions could be used to date the cloth to the first century were widely publicized and garnered both praise and criticism from the scientific community. Filas was also one of the founding members of the Holy Shroud Guild.

- *June 1, 1985:* At a meeting in Trondheim, Norway, Dr. Tite and Richard Burleigh of the British Museum, London, release the results of an inter-comparison experiment conducted between six radiocarbon dating laboratories, some using the old proportional counter method, others the new AMS method pioneered by Dr. Harry Gove. One of the samples was a 4,000-year-old Egyptian mummy wrapping for which one of the laboratories, Zurich, produced a 1000-year error due to faulty pre-treatment. Despite this gaffe, the experiment is seen as opening the way for a radiocarbon dating of the Shroud. Dr. Harry Gove sets in motion plans for a meeting of the six *laboratories and the British Museum to agree on a working procedure for the Shroud dating. It is suggested that the Pontifical Academy of Sciences be contacted.*

- *April 21, 1988: At 5 a.m. the Shroud is secretly taken out of its casket. At 6.30 a.m. Dr. Tite and the representatives of the three laboratories assemble at the cathedral. In the cathedral sacristy the Shroud is unrolled and shown to assembled representatives of the three chosen radiocarbon dating laboratories. Professor Testore of Turin Polytechnic, Gonella's choice as textile expert in place of Mme. Flury-Lemberg, reportedly asks 'What's that brown patch?' of the wound in the side. Professor Riggi and Professor Gonella reportedly spend two hours arguing about the exact location on the Shroud from which the sample should be taken. During the event, it is Riggi who seems in charge of the operation.*

  *At 9.45 a.m., with a video-camera recording his every move (he will later sell copies to international media and others), he cuts a sliver from one edge and divides this into two, then divides one of these halves into three. In a separate room (the Sala Capitolare), and now unrecorded by any camera, the Cardinal and Dr. Tite place these three latter samples in sealed canisters, for the respective laboratories to take away with them. At 1 p.m. the sample taking for carbon-dating purposes is formally completed, and the laboratory representatives depart.*

  *During the afternoon, and in the presence of some twenty witnesses, Riggi takes blood samples from the lower part of the crown-of-thorns bloodstains on the Shroud's dorsal image. Ac-*

*cording to Riggi's own subsequent account, he received the cardinal's permission to take for himself both these 'blood' samples and the portion of the Shroud he cut away but which was superfluous to the needs of the carbon-dating laboratories. These samples he will deposit in a bank vault. At 8.30 p.m. the Shroud is returned to its casket.*

Rosaria paused and took a deep breath. "This information is mind-boggling," she said. "I can't seem to take it all in."

"I'm sorry, I should've realized that," John said. "Let's have some more coffee and a quick bite before you read the rest – if you want to, that is."

"Of course I do," Rosaria sighed. "It's like stepping into a whole new world."

John knew exactly what she meant.

# Chapter 12
## (Day 3: midafternoon)

Rosaria replaced her cup, tucked her hair behind her ears, and smiled at John. "Those sandwiches were good. I'd like to go on now, if it's okay by you."

"By all means. You'll discover what followed the carbon dating – perhaps in greater detail than you anticipate," John warned her.

"And more about the mysterious deaths …?".

"That too," John assured her.

Rosaria flipped the page to continue reading:

- *May 6, 1988:* *9.50 am. In the presence of Professor Harry Gove, who has been invited to be present, the Shroud sample is run through the Arizona system. With the calibration applied, the date arrived at is 1350 AD.*

- *June 8, 1988:* *The Arizona laboratory completes*

*its work on the Shroud.*

- *Week of July 4, 1988:* *Having delayed because of technical adjustments to their radiocarbon dating unit, the Oxford laboratory begins its pretreatment of its Shroud sample and controls.*

- *July 15, 1988:* *At the Hotel Thalwiler Hof, Thalwil, Switzerland, Dr. Max Frei's entire collection of twenty-eight sticky-tape Shroud samples is formally handed over to the American Shroud group ASSIST.*

- *July 22, 1988:* *(Friday) Dr. Michael Tite of the British Museum receives the Zurich laboratory's radiocarbon dating findings.*

- *July 23, 1988:* *Shroud Meeting at the Academy of Natural Sciences, Philadelphia, in which Dr. Max Frei's sticky tape samples, just brought over from Europe, are formally and collectively studied by Dr. Walter McCrone, Dr. Alan Adler and others, under the auspices of the U.S. Shroud group ASSIST. This reveals that, in addition to pollens and fabric particles, the tapes bear a surprising proportion of plant parts and floral debris, suggesting that actual flowers were laid on the Shroud at some time during its history.*

- *July 27, 1988:* *(Wednesday) The Oxford laboratory commences its first run of its Shroud sample and controls.*

- *August 8, 1988:* *The Oxford laboratory completes its Shroud work.*

- *August 26, 1988:* *The London Evening Standard carries banner headlines declaring the Shroud to be a fake made in 1350. The source, Cambridge librarian Dr. Stephen Luckett, has no known previous connection with the Shroud, or with the carbon dating work, but in this article declares scientific laboratories 'leaky institutions'. The story is picked up around the world.*

- <u>September 18, 1988:</u> *Without quoting its source, The Sunday Times publishes a front-page story headlined: 'Official: The Turin Shroud is a Fake'. Professor Hall and Dr. Tite firmly deny any responsibility for this story.*

- <u>October 13, 1988:</u>*(Thursday) At a press conference held in Turin, Cardinal Ballestrero, Archbishop of Turin, makes an official announcement that the results of the three laboratories performing the carbon dating of the Shroud have determined an approximate 1325 date for the cloth. At a similar press conference held at the British Museum, London, it is announced that the Shroud dates between 1260 and 1390 AD. Newspaper headlines immediately brand the Shroud a fake and declare that the Catholic Church has accepted the results.*

- <u>April 28, 1989:</u> *Interviewed by journalists during a plane journey forming part of the papal visit to Africa, Pope John Paul II guardedly speaks of the Shroud as an authentic relic, while insisting that 'the Church has never pronounced on the matter'.*

- <u>June 4, 1989:</u> *Death of University of Arizona physicist Timothy W. Linick, one of the authors of the Nature report on the Shroud radiocarbon dating.*

- *September 30, 1989: New Scientist reports findings of the scientific workshop at East Kilbride that 'the margin of error with radiocarbon-dating ... may be two or three times as great as practitioners of the technique have claimed'.*

- *February 24, 1993: (Ash Wednesday) Because of the repairs to the Royal Chapel, the Shroud, without being taken out of its casket, is removed from its normal shrine in the Royal Chapel and transferred to a specially designed but temporary plate glass display case behind the High Altar, in the main body of Turin Cathedral. In poor health, Fr. Peter Rinaldi has flown from the States to be present at this transfer, but collapses and is taken to a Turin hospital.*

- *February 28, 1993: Death of Fr. Peter Rinaldi, one of the co-founders of the Holy Shroud Guild and, along with Frs. Adam Otterbein and Francis Filas, among the main people responsible for helping STURP obtain permission to perform their examination of the Shroud in 1978.*

- *December 14, 1995: Death of Dr. John Heller, who, with Dr. Alan Adler, made a detailed study of the chemistry of the Shroud body image and blood image samples taken by the STURP team in 1978. In 1983, Heller authored 'Report on the Shroud of Turin', a book about the STURP team's examination of the Shroud that included a summary of their findings.*

- *April 11 & 12, 1997: Shortly after 11 p.m., fire breaks out in Turin's Guarini Chapel, quickly threatening the Shroud's bulletproof display case. Fireman Mario Trematore uses a sledgehammer to break open this case and the Shroud, in its traditional casket, is taken temporarily to Cardinal Saldarini's residence. Signs of arson are found in the Royal Chapel, the walls of which are very badly damaged. Also damaged are the whole High Altar end of the cathedral and the part of the Royal Palace directly adjoining the Chapel.*

- *April 14, 1997:* *In the presence of the Cardinal and several invited specialists, including Mme. Flury-Lemberg, Professor Baima-Bollone and Dr. Rosalia Piazza of Rome's Istituto Centrale del Restauro, the Shroud is brought out from its casket and its condition carefully examined. It is found to be completely unaffected by the fire. It is taken to an undisclosed place of safety.*

- *April 18 to June 14, 1998:* *Public exposition of the Shroud is held to commemorate the centenary of Secondo Pia's first photograph of the cloth, the discovery of its hidden negative image and the beginning of the scientific era of its study. Over two million pilgrims visit the Shroud during the eight-week exhibition.*

- *May 24, 1998:* *Pope John Paul II visits the Shroud as it is displayed in the Cathedral of St. John the Baptist, in Turin. The visit occurs on the exact day that Secondo Pia made the first photograph of the Shroud 100 years earlier, on May 24, 1898. This is the first time the Pope has seen the cloth since a private viewing in 1980.*

- *June 15, 1998:* *Death of Father Adam J. Otterbein, C.Ss.R., founder of the Holy Shroud Guild.*

- *June 21, 1998:* *Death of Cardinal Anastasio Alberto Ballestrero, Archbishop of Turin from*

*1978 to 1989. Responsible for giving STURP permission to perform their scientific examination in October 1978, he was still Archbishop in 1988 when Shroud samples were taken and the controversial radiocarbon 14 dating was performed that concluded the Shroud was of medieval origin.*

- *January 22, 1999: An article in the Frankfurter Allgemeine Zeitung (FAZ), a major newspaper in Frankfurt, Germany, announces the discovery of a previously unknown, precise copy of the Shroud of Turin in the West Bohemian Benedictine Monastery at Broumov, Czechloslovakia. The copy is accompanied by a letter of authenticity signed by the Archbishop of Turin, dated 4 May 1651.*

- *March 4, 1999: Rodger J. Apple, founder of the Albany Chapter Turin Shroud (ACTUS), dies at his home in Albany, New York, after a long illness.*

- *November 10, 1999: Roger A. Morris, original member of the STURP team that examined the Shroud in 1978, dies at his home in White Rock, New Mexico, after a short illness.*

- *June 10, 2000: Dr. Alan Adler, world-renowned chemist, original STURP team member and one of the most important scientists in international sindonology, dies unexpectedly in his sleep. His death rocks the world of Shroud research to its foundations. Adler was the only American scientist on Archbishop of Turin Saldarini's Scientific Advisory Commission. His loss is mourned worldwide and is considered by many as a serious blow to American Shroud research.*

- *October 14, 2000:* *Don Lynn, imaging expert from the Jet Propulsion Laboratory and original STURP team member, dies unexpectedly in his sleep. Again the world of sindonology mourns the loss of one of its most well respected researchers.*

- *September 19, 2001:* *Dr. Robert Bucklin, world renowned forensic pathologist, original STURP team member and sindonologist with more than 50 years of Shroud research to his credit, dies in Ft. Myers Beach, Florida, U.S.A.*

- *July 10, 2002:* *Death of Walter McCrone, probably the world's most well known Shroud skeptic; he was the first modern scientific researcher to publicly proclaim the Shroud of Turin a 'beautiful painting'. Although he was a proponent of the painting theory since 1979 and published many articles supporting this theory, he ironically made a significant contribution to sindonological research, since his work spawned countless studies worldwide, in art, chemistry, hematology and history, all aimed at challenging his conclusions. Interestingly, at the time of his death, the Shroud was undergoing a major 'restoration' in Turin (see below).*

- *June 20 - July 22, 2002:* *A small group of textile experts, headed by Mechtild Fleury-Lemberg of Switzerland, perform a dramatic and radical 'restoration' of the Shroud under the auspices of the Archbishop of Turin and his advisors at the Turin Center for Shroud Studies, and with the full permission of the Vatican. They remove the thirty patches sewn into the cloth by Poor Clare nuns in 1534 to repair burn holes from the 1532 fire. They remove the backing cloth (frequently referred to as the 'Holland Cloth') that was sewn onto the back of the Shroud in 1534 to strengthen the fire-damaged relic. They photograph the hidden backside of the cloth and then re-attach a new, whiter linen backing cloth. They use lead weights suspended from the edges of the Shroud to 'flatten' many of the creases in the cloth and apply steam to certain areas to help accomplish this. They handle the cloth without gloves or special clothing. They scrape away the charred edges of all the burned areas and collect the scrapings into small containers. During a continuous period of thirty-two days, they expose the cloth to significant amounts of potentially damaging light and the polluted air of Turin. They perform this restoration in secret, without consulting any of the world's Shroud experts (including most of their own advisors) that could have contributed important scientific guidance to ensure that no valuable scientific or historical data was lost or damaged during the restoration. They set off a firestorm of controversy, criticism, debate and recrimination that ultimately engulfs, polarizes and divides the Shroud research community.*

Watching Rosaria frown in concentration, John interrupted her scan of the history pages.

"If you want more information on how this important event unfolded, you could check the 2002 Website News page at shroud.com. You will also want to read the 'Comments on the Restoration' page, where fourteen noted Shroud experts express their own opinions of the restoration."

"I'm stupefied by the amount of information," said Rosaria. "It's a phenomenal account."

"That it is," John agreed.

"Just before he passed away earlier this year," he continued, "Raymond N. Rogers ... but that's right there," he broke off, pointing to the page. "You can read it for yourself."

Rosaria nodded her appreciation and returned to the pages she held.

- *<u>January 20, 2005:</u> A peer-reviewed scientific paper by Raymond N. Rogers, retired Fellow of the Los Alamos National Laboratory, is published in the journal Thermochimica Acta, Volume 425, Issues 1-2, Pages 189-194. Titled 'Studies on the radiocarbon sample from the Shroud of Turin', the paper concludes: 'As unlikely as it seems, the sample used to test the age of the Shroud of Turin in 1988 was taken from a rewoven area of the Shroud. Pyrolysis-mass spectrometry results from the sample area coupled with microscopic and microchemical observations prove that the radiocarbon sample was not part of the original cloth of the Shroud of Turin. The radiocarbon date was thus not valid for determining the true age of the Shroud'.*

Rosaria drew in a deep breath as she folded the thick sheaf of papers and carefully put it in her bag. Her eyes were slightly glazed as she looked up at him gratefully. "Thank you so much, John. There's no way I'd have located all this information on my own. I just hope," she added, "I haven't taken up too much of your time."

John looked at his watch; it was 2.30 pm. The hours had flown by.

"Let me give you a set of the Shroud interview CDs to take home. I think you'll be impressed with the depth of the STURP group's research. Tomorrow is the first day of the convention, so I'll be tied up until sometime in the afternoon. Perhaps we could get together with Victor and go over what we know about the mysterious disappearance of the casket?"

"What are your plans for this evening?" she asked. "I hope you don't mind my asking?"

"Nothing planned," he replied. "What did you have in mind?"

"Two of my closest friends, Brian and Lola Parsons, are international illusionists and they're making a rare appearance here in Malta. They're just back from a hugely successful tour of Spain that I'll be reporting on. I thought you might like to catch their act. I just had a crazy idea that they might have some thoughts on our mysterious disappearance – if you don't mind me discussing it with them, that is?"

"Of course not, that sounds like a great idea," John said. "I'll just check if it's okay with Victor, though," he added. "What time should I be ready? You know, this will be quite a treat for me. I'm deeply interested in illusion and magic. I've enjoyed visiting the Magic Castle in L.A. on several occasions. In fact, I once recorded a live television broadcast from there."

"Really? You must tell me more about it. I'm sure Brian and Lola will be interested too. I'll pick you up around 7, if that's okay."

"Sounds good, Rosaria. I'll be ready."

"Please," she replied, "call me Rose. Everybody does!"

John leant forward and kissed her gently on the cheek as he escorted her to the door.

For some reason, he felt drained and yet strangely excited at the prospect of the evening ahead. He stretched out on the bed and immediately fell asleep.

## Chapter 13
### (Day 3: late afternoon)

It was about 5.30 when John awoke. He showered and dressed for his unexpected evening out with Rosaria and then picked up the phone to dial Victor's number.

"Hi, Victor," John greeted his old friend. "Just spent a wonderful day with your niece. You were quite right, she certainly is a delightful young lady and, by the way, very concerned about you."

"Yes, she's the best," Victor agreed. "A very smart head on those pretty shoulders."

"You're right. I was impressed by her very real interest in the history of the Shroud. By the way," he added, "we're planning to see a show together tonight. She's going to introduce me to some friends of hers who she feels may be able to help us with the problem we currently face. I assume you would have no objection to my discussing the disappearance with them?"

"I know I can rely on your discretion, John." Victor sounded pleased that he had connected with Rosaria. "We'll meet again tomorrow, I guess?"

"Sometime in the afternoon, if that's okay?"

"Fine," Victor replied. "I look forward to it."

\*\*\*

The Mellieha Hotel sits facing south on the edge of one of Malta's most popular beaches at Mellieha Bay, at the northern end of the island. Brian and Lola turned out to be a delightful couple. They had just returned from a six-month tour of Spain and were, as Rosaria had said, making one of their rare local appearances.

It appeared from their conversation that evening that there was a very active magic society on the island – surprising, John thought, for such a small community. It was easy to see why Rosaria's friends had been so successful in Spain. For the next hour and a half, John forgot the problems and mysteries that, in some strange way, now involved him. He sat entranced by Brian and Lola's performance. Items vanished and re appeared, a table floated in mid-air. The effect, although John knew it was an illusion, never failed to baffle him. As the crowds dispersed, John and Rosaria sat deep in conversation, awaiting the arrival of the two star performers.

John took an immediate liking to Brian and they chatted effortlessly about magic, travel and – finally – the missing casket.

Brian was intrigued by the disappearance. As he and Lola had just returned from several months overseas, he had heard nothing of the mysterious disappearance of a silver chest from the sacred grotto at St. Paul's.

"What was in it that made it so important?" Brian asked.

## In the Image of His God

John hesitated. "Some very valuable documents relating to the St. Paul's Mission and the saint's shipwreck here in Malta." He hoped he sounded convincing.

"Wow!" said Brian. "I can understand the church's concern. St. Paul is considered the patron saint of the island!"

John explained to Brian exactly what he knew of the mysterious disappearance, the locked gates that were supposed to have protected it and Father Victor's deep anguish at losing an item personally entrusted to him by His Holiness.

"I'm not sure what we can contribute," Brian said, glancing at Lola, who nodded, "but we would be delighted to help in any way you feel we can."

"What I suggest," John replied, "is that we meet tomorrow at the grotto and go over what we know together. Perhaps you'll see something we overlooked."

"That sounds like a good idea. What time do you have in mind – Lola and I are free all day."

"I suggest about 3.30. That should give us plenty of time before they close the gates."

"Great! We'll see you then," Brian said, as they bid their farewells.

John and Rosaria made little conversation on the drive back to John's hotel. They had both had a long day.

"I'll try to find time to review the CDs you gave me before I see you tomorrow. What time should we meet? Would you like me to pick you up from your hotel?" Rosaria asked as John got out of her car.

"If it's not inconvenient for you, I'll be at the Conference Center. How about lunch, say 12.30?"

"Sounds good," she said. "And no problem – I'll pick you up at the Center."

"Goodnight, Rose, and thank you for a wonderful evening," John said, leaning into her window and giving her an affectionate peck on her cheek. "Tomorrow at 12.30 then. Goodnight," he said again. He watched as her taillights disappeared around the corner.

# Chapter 14
## (Day 4: morning)

John awoke knowing he had a busy day ahead. He would attend the early sessions of the convention before meeting Rosaria at 12.30 for lunch. A message on his hotel messaging service told him that Brian would be coming alone. Something unexpected had cropped up, needing Lola's attention.

John finished his breakfast and caught a cab to the Mediterranean Conference Center. Despite his interest in the subjects under discussion, his thoughts and mind were elsewhere. This was the last day of the convention and he felt guilty about not having attended more sessions. Tonight he would be the feature speaker at the closing dinner. If the delegates only knew that they were not only in a land where the Shroud once was, but where it was now hidden away somewhere … What a story *that* would make!

At 12.30 sharp, John was waiting for Rosaria outside the Center. She arrived promptly to collect him for lunch. He had selected Bacchus, a unique restaurant nestled within the walled city of M'dina, a place that had been recommended to him by the American Ambassador when they met at the convention a couple of days earlier. M'dina was only a few minutes from St. Agatha's and John had wanted to visit the old city once more; this was a good opportunity.

During the short drive to M'dina, they first went over the details of the mystery of the missing casket. Rosaria spent the rest of the drive complimenting John on the interview recordings he had given her last night. Dr. Walter McCrone particularly impressed her. Walter's had been the only dissenting voice amongst the investigating team. John was quick to point out to her that Dr. McCrone had not been present during the STURP group's investigations. She was obviously keenly interested, as she bombarded John with a stream of questions. As she parked the car outside the walled city, she brought up the subject of the blood specimens.

"You'll have to listen to the full transcripts, and even then I doubt you'll be less puzzled," John remarked, as they moved through the city gates.

The Bacchus Restaurant was tucked away in a narrow side street of the ancient capital. It was just as the Ambassador had described it. As much of the original building that could be retained in its commercial configuration had been restored to its former glory. The décor reflected the bacchanalian motif, with giant silver goblets along the walls, lights with antique copper-finish leaves on the walls and ceiling, and classical portraits.

They chatted easily over a four-course lunch, discussing their work, Brian and Lola, and Victor's magnificent contribution to St. Agatha's. It seemed no time before they were hastily making their way to St. Agatha's to meet with Victor and Brian.

After the formal introductions were taken care of, the group moved to the crypt and the secret passage to the grotto. Although Brian had visited the catacombs as a schoolboy, he had little recollection of the vast array of tunnels and the enormous number and varying types of graves that existed. Like so many of his fellow Maltese, he had never explored the archaeological treasures that abounded on the tiny island. Father Victor gave Brian a brief lesson as they made their way to the grotto.

"The different types of tombs are another feature that distinguishes the Maltese catacombs."

"I want to hear this too," Rosaria linked her arm in Victor's.

"John and I will tell you what we can. This was our major discovery, all those years ago," he said, patting her hand. "Let me begin with the tombs. The most important of all is the 'saddle-back canopied table grave'. The upper part of the tomb, what you might call the cover, is like a saddleback marking on a horse. It was either cut from the same rock or was placed when the internment took place. Four short pillars ending in arches on the four sides support the canopy above. At the back of each pillar, on the internal side of the tomb, there are decorative markings in the form of horn-like pillars."

"Another type of grave," John went on, "is the 'canopied table grave', known as *tomba a baldacchino* in Italian. These are also cut in the rock and have four pillars to support the ceiling above, while forming arches on each side of the tomb. These make a sort of canopy above the grave. When the funeral was over and the grave sealed with stone slabs, it seemed to form a table, hence its name. Then there's the arcosolium. Have I got that right, Victor?"

"As if you wouldn't!" Victor said, turning around to smile at his old friend. "The arcosolium is so called because at the entrance of the tomb, it has an arch and a sill – *solium* in Latin. Such graves are carved into the sidewalls. The back of the arch is a sort of half-dome. The entrance to these graves is through a square opening about 1.5 feet on each side, while the wall hides the grave itself.

"Window graves are very similar to the arcosolium, except that the back is flat within the vault. The entrance is also similar.

"Loculi are side graves hewn in the sidewalls. Most of these were meant for children and babies. At times, many of these are found near each other and very near to a parent tomb, indicating that they belong to the same family."

"Small niches can be seen cut in the sidewalls," John added. These were most probably used to hold an oil lamp to light the catacomb and many niches bear soot marks to this day."

They gazed about them, awed by the age-old marvels. "I'm sorry Lola couldn't make it today," Rosaria said to Brian. "She'd have loved hearing about this."

"I certainly intend to bring her back here soon. This place is amazing!"

Father Victor gestured them to silence as they approached the roll-away stone entrance and listened to make sure the guides had left. It was just after 4.30 and it had been a slow day. The guards had actually closed up the iron gates fifteen minutes earlier. The lights were still on; however, the red light indicating that the CCTV was operating was off. Victor pointed out to Brian the location where the casket had been stored at the foot of the statue of St. Paul.

"We're faced with two mysteries as I see it, Brian. One: how did the thief get access through the sealed and locked gates? Two: if he carried out the theft during the time the catacombs are open to the public, how was he not seen by the CCTV camera?" John asked.

Brian, though equally unskilled at the art of crime detection as anyone else present, started by examining the locks on the gates. There were two, and neither looked tampered with, though their age made any real determination almost impossible.

"It would appear to me that our intruder either entered during the hours this area was open to the public or was aware of the passage we just used," Brian commented. "The keys to these locks are so ancient that I doubt one could have a duplicate made without arousing suspicion."

Brian turned his attention to the CCTV camera. Walking over to it, he gazed up at the securing bracket that held the camera to the wall.

"Is there something I can stand on?" he asked.

Victor picked up the guides' stool that was beside the gate and brought it over to Brian.

Perched on the stool, Brian looked closely at the bracket. Running his finger along the bracket, he remarked, "There has recently been duct tape applied to this area. The adhesive is still reasonably fresh, not more that a couple of weeks old, I'd guess."

John and Victor moved closer and Rosaria helped support them as all three tried to balance rather precariously on the stool.

"What possible connection could that have?" Victor asked Brian.

"Well, Father, some years ago I performed an illusion on television that involved the disappearance of the Pyramid of Cheops in Egypt," Brian said. "The live audience saw nothing disappear; however, the television audience saw what they believed to be the vanishing of the Pyramid before their very eyes. The effect was achieved by slipping a picture of the scene, with the Pyramid retouched out, in front of the camera lens at the appropriate moment. The frame that held the picture was taped to the camera tripod and supported by a long stick, placing the picture far enough away from the lens to keep it, and myself – who stood to the side – in focus."

John said, "So you're suggesting that the thief effectively blocked out the attendant's view and all that would be seen on the monitor would be the casket still in place? That is, if anyone was watching the monitor at the time."

"Exactly!" Brian said. "If he was unaware of the security procedures or had any doubt, it would be a wise precaution. He – or she –," he added, flashing Rosaria a grin, "would have been free to remove the casket and return later to remove the picture and its support."

John considered the ruse. He knew only too well how the most ingenious magic tricks and illusions were based on principles that seemed ridiculously simple when explained. "Well, if that's the case," he said, "I feel sure he entered through the tunnel after the gates were closed and the guards well out of the way." Victor and Rosaria nodded in agreement.

"It appears that we seem to be dealing with a rather clever individual, and we've narrowed the possibilities to someone who may not only have known about the secret passage but had access to the crypt," Victor said. "John, it's getting late and I know you have a dinner to attend. Perhaps we should adjourn our get-together until tomorrow morning? I want to contemplate and pray about this new discovery. Thank you Brian, you've been a great help. Perhaps I can arrange to see your show one day? Rosaria speaks highly of your performance."

"Thank you, Father. It would be my pleasure," Brian remarked, as they made their way back to Victor's office.

"I've invited Rosaria to accompany me to the dinner tonight, Victor. I know how you hate to go anywhere after dark. I invited Brian as well, but unfortunately he has a show to do. What time should we meet tomorrow?"

"If it's alright with you, John, may I call you in the morning when I've had a chance to think this whole thing over once again, especially in light of Brian's deductions?"

"Of course, Victor, that'd be fine. Not too early, though. It could be a late night with the closing ceremony of the convention," John said, as he clasped his friend's frail hand in farewell.

Rosaria dropped John at his hotel and arranged to pick him up again at 7.30. It would be a short drive to Valletta for the convention's closing dinner and they both needed time to get into formal gear.

\*\*\*

What with adding the final touches to his speech and contacting the curator of the Wignacourt Museum about his proposed work on the Rabat Shroud, John just about managed to be ready when Rosaria arrived to pick him up. He couldn't believe the transformation in her – she looked like a film star attending the Oscars! He, on the other hand, had never liked dressing up for these occasions, though protocol demanded it. Rosaria remarked on how handsome he looked. Oh, how he wished he were forty years younger!

John rose to a standing ovation after he was introduced to the assembled delegates and Maltese officials.

"Honored guests, ladies and gentlemen of the Shroud Society and members of the press," John began, smiling at Rosaria seated beside him. "I cannot begin to tell you what an honor and absolute delight it has been to set foot once again on my beloved Malta."

John dearly wanted to criticize the present Department of Heritage, responsible for the care and protection of the historical sites on the Maltese Islands. Even in the short time he had been back on the island, it seemed to him that the efforts of the government were pitiful, at best. He saw the Minister for Tourism in the audience and thought better of it. It would serve little purpose, and most likely achieve nothing. Instead, he devoted his time to recapping his historic interviews and, more importantly, his discovery of the Shroud of Rabat, located in a seldom-visited alcove in the Wignacourt Museum. "I will be working with Father Muscat, the curator of the Wignacourt Museum, to restore the Rabat Shroud. It is to be remounted and exhibited in a more prominent place. In fact, some of you may want to stay behind for the opening ceremony, to be held in a few days' time."

John waited for the low buzz of conversation that greeted this announcement to die down. "We find such reproductions in several countries," he continued. "In Belgium, Argentina, France, Portugal, Spain and Italy."

He held up a copy of the article he had obtained from the museum.

*"The information I'm going to share with you is from an article by Brother Michael Buttigieg, F.S.C., who discusses a reproduction of the Holy Shroud of Turin in Rabat, measuring* 293.5 by 101 cm. The frame is 7 cm wide. Research is still being conducted on the Shroud of Rabat, but there is no doubt that has been authenticated by the Archbishop of Turin, Michael Beyamus, in 1663. This is his testimony:

'To all and every person living at present or in the future, we attest and in truth declare that on the fifteenth day of last May, when the Most Sacred Shroud in which the Most Sacred Body of Christ had been placed by Joseph of Arimathea (which without any doubt is kept in our Metropolitan Church in the Royal Chapel) was being shown to the large number of people frequenting the Church, in the presence of the King of the State of Savoy, the above drawn image herewith attached, was moved near the original Most Sacred Shroud and We made it touch it and We guarded it.'

"This document is dated June 20 1663," John said, looking around at his audience. "It is signed and certified by Archbishop Michele Beyamus and countersigned by Neromi, probably the Notary of the Archdiocese of Turin.

"You may wonder why I am bringing this article to your notice. As the author of this article has pointed out, it gives us two valuable pieces of information about the Shroud of Rabat.

"First, the date of its public exhibition, called *ostensione*, is given as 15 May 1663. Second, the Shroud of Rabat was made to touch the Holy Shroud of Turin and sanctified by the holiest of holy relics. So far, this is all we know about the Rabat Shroud when it was still in Turin."

John paused for a drink of water, and looked up at the hushed audience. "No more is known about it for the next nineteen years. The next mention of the Rabat Shroud is in the 'Account Books' preserved in the St. Paul's Grotto Archives, which reveal that on 13 April 1682 two men transported the frame of the most holy Shroud from Valletta to Rabat for the princely sum of 4 scudi." He waited for the subdued laughter to die down before he continued.

"On the following day, Master Guglielmo Alfart was paid 5 scudi for measuring and fixing these frames in the sacristy of St. Publius."

Sensing that he had his audience's undivided attention, John decided to continue. "Over a half-century later, in 1756, the General Inventory under the section 'Furniture of the Sacrestia' records a description of the frame. This attestation is repeated in the subsequent inventory of 1779.

"So far, so good, but several questions remain unanswered. When was the Rabat Shroud brought to Malta? Who brought it? Who received it? What veneration was it given? More patient research may give the answer to these and similar questions."

*John folded the sheet of paper he had been reading from as he made eye contact with his audience. "I would highly recommend," he said, "that all of you take the opportunity to visit the Rabat Shroud before leaving the island. It may be as close as many of us will come to the real Shroud within our lifetime and is an opportunity not to be missed. It may, in fact, inspire the present administration to provide the kind of exposure and protection that such a great relic deserves. I thank you for this opportunity to address you all and wish you a pleasant stay on this magnificent island."*

*As John took his seat, the assembled body rose to their feet as one and gave him a well-deserved ovation that lasted several minutes. Rosaria felt very proud to be at John's side. She knew Victor would also have loved to be present.*

As they mingled with the other participants, John wondered what Victor was doing, and whether Brian's discovery had eased his mind or agitated it even more.

# Chapter 15
(Day 4: late evening)

Long after John and the others had left, Victor remained at his desk, thinking of their discussion. It was certainly good to have someone to confide in. He had missed his old friend over the years. During the five short years they had worked together they had become very close, one of those inexplicable bonds that last a lifetime. Victor had been saddened when their contact all but ceased, as John got involved in other fields of endeavor. Had he done right in getting him involved in this bizarre mystery? He wished his failing eyesight had not prevented him from attending John's closing speech to the visiting convention.

As Victor pondered Brian's conclusion, he tried to think of who else might be aware of the little-known passage leading to the grotto. Brother Darren immediately came to mind.

*What about Brother Darren?* he thought. *He may be a misguided young man, but is he really capable of doing something like this? I'm sure he has many redeeming qualities. Could he have taken the casket thinking the contents were what I have told the world at large, just historical papers pertaining to St. Paul's shipwreck on the Is-*

# In the Image of His God

*land of Malta?*

He knew he was tired and should head for bed, but his brain refused to cooperate, pummeling his mind with questions. *And if he has taken the casket, how? The gates were locked! As far as I know, the young man doesn't know about the secret entrance. And even if he stole the casket during the day, why did no one see him? So many unanswered questions ...*

Leaning heavily against his desk as he arose, Father Victor took a key from his cassock to open a small safe in the corner of his office and proceeded to remove a plastic envelope containing papers. Among them were two envelopes, one of which bore the papal seal; the other was open and showed signs of its great age.

For a long time, Victor stared at the package, his brow creased with worry. Finally, he slipped it into his inside pocket and left his office. He made his way from the museum to his quarters in the main building.

As he entered, he saw a light under Brother Darren's door. This was unusual; novices were encouraged to retire early. As he approached the door, he became even more perplexed. There were voices emanating from the room. Novices were strictly forbidden from having visitors in their rooms, other than on open days – and even then, only close family.

Victor slowed his pace to a shuffle as he edged toward the closed door. The voices were raised in anger and Victor immediately recognized Brother Darren's. He could hear only snatches of conversation.

"Please ... very difficult ... a mistake to ... " That was young Darren, his voice pitched high.

"No choice ... taking too long ... as discussed." The stranger's voice was low and menacing. It suddenly rose in volume and the next few words stopped Victor in his tracks!

"How often do I have to repeat myself? The Illuminati does not take kindly to dissenters. You made a commitment. You have been paid. We shall expect delivery as agreed!"

Victor heard heavy footsteps move towards the door. Much as he wanted to see the face of the intruder, he did not want to be seen. Moving as fast as he could, he walked quickly away toward his room across the hall. The light from Brother Darren's opening door flashed across the hall, illuminating his entry into his room, but he dared not turn. Had they seen him, he wondered, his heart throbbing, the blood pounding in his ears. He shakily lowered himself to his bed.

For hours he lay awake. *The Illuminati! What on earth has young Darren got himself into now? More important, what at St. Agatha's can possibly be of interest to that notorious group?*

Victor had read much about the workings of this secret society. Determined as they were supposed to be to overthrow the Catholic Church, he had never heard mention of their presence on the tiny island of Malta.

The first published proof of the Illuminati appeared around 1789 – a secret society of powerful individuals whose goal was to replace all world religions with what they described as humanism. As Victor understood the movement, it rejects a divine authority and proposes a single world-dominating government through assassination, bribery and blackmail. By moving their principal members into positions of power in world governments, banks, and even the Church, they intend to ultimately be in a position of global domination. There is no question that the largest body of people on our planet is today influenced by one great power, the Catholic Church! Anything that discredited the Church and possibly led to its downfall from grace would greatly further their interests and eventual goal.

"My God!" Victor exclaimed aloud. "The Shroud! It *has* to be that! They've discovered the real contents of the casket!"

Victor's head was spinning. Had the Illuminati found out about the switch? Did they know about the holy relic's arrival in Malta? There was no doubt that the secret society had infiltrated the Vatican, but could they have managed to insinuate a member into the inner circle that enjoyed the Pope's confidence? Who could he tell, what should he do? Victor dropped to his knees in prayer.

"Holy Father, I beseech you to guide me at this time. Father, grant me the wisdom and strength to carry out your work. Show me that which I must do to preserve your holy relic and keep it from the hands of the infidels."

Victor remained in prayer for over an hour before rising and moving to his writing desk.

*Dear John,* he wrote.

*I am enclosing two envelopes, which I do not feel safe entrusting to anyone other than you. The one contains His Holiness's authority for my possession of the object we seek; and the other is the original Da Vinci letter that was in the possession of Father Rinaldi until it was given to His Holiness."* He purposely did not mention the Holy Shroud.

*Tonight I have discovered a plot that I believe is intended to bring discredit to the office of the Holy See and ultimately to the Church. I believe the Illuminati may be responsible for the disappearance of the silver casket! I now know that Brother Darren is involved. Just how and to what extent, I intend to find out. In view of the possible risks involved I am having this document delivered by hand to your hotel tonight. Hopefully, I will have more answers for you when we meet tomorrow.*

Victor read the letter to himself before enclosing it in an envelope with the two documents he had removed from his cupboard. He sealed it and addressed the envelope to 'Dr. John Peters, Room #235, Radisson SAS Hotel, St. Julian's Bay', and marked it URGENT. He then called a cab service they frequently used for delivering documents or messages within the church community and handed over the envelope for delivery.

He would confront Brother Darren before prayers in the morning. He looked at his watch. It was 1.30 am. He should try and get some sleep.

***

As Brother Darren opened the door to allow his guest to leave, he observed Father Victor disappearing into his room. Had he overheard any of their conversation?

Had he heard the threats that his visitor had made? Could he possibly be aware that he had stolen the silver casket? Thoughts churned relentlessly through his mind.

He was not an overly bright young man. He came from a dysfunctional family and was brought up in the small seaside township of G'zira, which lay halfway between the capital of Valetta and the tourist center of Sliema. His parents had both found new relationships but continued to live under one roof. Divorce was not possible on the island.

His final years of schooling had been at the Selvatico Boys' School in Naxxar, an education facility that focused more on real-life skills and less on academic qualifications. It was his headmaster who had suggested St. Agatha's. There was still doubt in his unsettled mind as to his path in life; that is, until he was approached by a friend of his old headmaster who had offered him a possible alternative to a life of religious service.

He had been approached by the stranger – till this day, he didn't know his name – at a small café just outside M'dina. The stranger seemed to know all about him, but disclosed nothing about himself. He told Darren it was not necessary to use names but to focus on the mission at hand. He belonged, he said, to a sacred order dedicated to the furthering of mankind. If Brother Darren would help them obtain an item that was rightfully theirs, he would be paid a handsome sum, and he would be offered a position of some note in the order he represented. It was some time later that Darren found out the order was the Illuminati. It would have made little difference, as Brother Darren had no idea who the Illuminati were or what exactly they stood for.

"10,000 lire!" Darren exclaimed, when the stranger had told him what he would receive. That was three years' salary for most young men on the island. The item they required was one that had held a fascination for Darren since it had arrived on the island: a simple silver casket that bore the papal seal. The casket purportedly contained letters and documents that related to St. Paul's shipwreck on the island. It had been given to Father Victor for safe keeping by none other than the Holy See himself. The novice had been present when the silver casket was placed at the foot of the statue of St. Paul in the grotto beneath the Church of St. Paul, where the saint was said to have lived during the three months he preached on the island.

The reward was too great and too much of a temptation! Brother Darren agreed to procure the silver casket.

In the two months since he had been assigned to assist Father Victor, he had got to know the old priest's every move. From his room opposite Victor's, he had seen the elderly priest slip out late at night on several occasions, and on one occasion had followed him as he made his way to the secret passage and the entrance to the grotto. To the young novice, Father Victor's devotion to the Holy Father's gift had not seemed odd. He had watched as Father Victor knelt in prayer before the statue of St. Paul.

He had long since made the decision to leave the priesthood. It seemed that fate had smiled on him when the stranger appeared out of nowhere with the chance of a lifetime – the opportunity to finance his re-entry into the real world. He must be careful, though. The money would be of little use if he ended up in jail. In this tiny Catholic country, the authorities had no mercy on perpetrators of crimes against the Church.

He would need time to make plans. He had told his mystery benefactor that he would need at least a week or two to accomplish his mission.

He wanted to take no chances. He found it difficult to think of a foolproof plan till he remembered a successful ploy in a movie he had recently seen. Taking a photograph of the casket in place at the foot of the statue of St. Paul did not involve much effort. He intended to place the picture in front of the security camera, just in case it was still active after the receptionist had left. This way, the monitor would continue to show the crypt empty and he would be free to remove the casket unobserved.

He had planned to take the casket immediately after Father Victor's visit early that Thursday. However, for reasons unknown to the young novice, Father Victor changed his scheduled early-morning visit. Brother Darren sat up all night waiting for Father Victor to make the usual pilgrimage to the grotto, but Victor never left his room that night.

Darren began to worry about losing his nerve. *If the deed has to be done, it's best done now, this very day,* he told himself. He hastily revised his plan. He would enter the grotto via the secret passage after 5 pm, when the guards left for the day. His plan was to secrete the casket in a canopy grave within the closed passages that led to the grotto. Besides Father Victor's secret visits, no one entered this area and, with no lighting, it would be easy to conceal the casket and keep it hidden.

\*\*\*

Everything had gone according to plan. Brother Darren had waited patiently behind the removable stone that sealed the entrance, until he heard the guard lock the iron gates that secured the grotto. He had waited a further twenty minutes before silently slipping into the grotto, making sure he was out of the range of the CCTV camera. He had placed the photograph he had taken the week earlier on a short stick so that it protruded about two feet in front of the camera lens. This would give an image almost indistinguishable from the one on the reception monitor.

He had slid beneath the camera, sprung onto the guide's stool that he has positioned carefully beneath it, and, with one swift move, taped the stick to the base of the camera mount. He had been extra careful to ensure that any perceived movement would look like a simple flicker on the monitor. Picture securely in place, he had carefully lifted the silver casket into his arms and returned to the passage. He would return momentarily to remove the picture and any evidence of his visit.

Placing the casket in a dun-colored pillowslip he had left in the canopy grave, he proceeded to cover it with the loose earth and bone fragments that still filled the base of the grave. This accomplished, he had returned swiftly to the grotto and removed the picture using the same caution he had taken on its installation. Holding the stick securely, he had removed the duct tape, replaced the stool, and left the grotto, re-sealing the doorway as he left.

Almost two weeks had passed since that night and Brother Darren had got little sleep.

He had visited his ill-gotten treasure on several occasions, but never dared to break the papal seal and venture a peek inside.

Something was terribly wrong. Instead of elation at accomplishing his assigned task and making more money than most young men made over several years, he was filled with remorse! He had seen the terrible effect that the missing casket had had on Father Victor. Although he had been working with the aging priest for only a few months, he could not forget how gracious Victor had been on discovering his novice's indiscretion when he tried to steal the valuable stamps. Brother Darren knew full well that Victor had been aware of his crime. Despite his dissatisfaction, he knew that the members of St. Agatha's were, for all intents and purposes, his only real family.

He had managed to keep the Illuminati at bay until the unscheduled visit this evening. The envelope containing 10,000 lire still lay unopened under his pillow.

# Chapter 16
## (Day 5: early morning)

After having tossed and turned without being able to sleep, the stranger's menacing words still echoing in his mind, Brother Darren rose early and made his way to the canopy grave where he had concealed the silver casket. Almost involuntarily, he found himself kneeling in prayer.

Victor, who had barely managed four hours' broken sleep, felt a deep compulsion to pray at the sacred grotto. He felt it would bring him some measure of comfort. As he emerged from his room, he just caught a glimpse of young Darren moving swiftly in the direction of the crypt. He was about to call out to him, when he decided it might be better to follow the novice.

To Victor's amazement, the young man was heading in the direction of the secret passage. Victor quietly followed him to the canopy grave. He stood silently in the shadows and watched as Darren withdrew the pillowcase from inside the grave. He witnessed the novice kneeling in prayer and waited, silent and motionless.

Darren rose. He picked up the pillowcase and was about to remove the silver casket when Father Victor made his move. Striding forward with all the authority he could muster, he reached for the pillowcase. Startled at being discovered, Brother Darren pulled away violently, crashing backward into the support beam that had been the subject of John's concern the previous day.

There was an almighty crashing sound and a huge cloud of dust and gravel as the roadway above subsided into the catacomb below. Father Victor was instantly pinned beneath the falling beam and lay motionless and unconscious. Brother Darren was not so lucky. A slab of concrete from above smashed into his skull, hurling him to the ground. He died instantly. The silver casket, still wrapped in the pillowcase, rolled back toward the canopy grave opening as if returning to the sanctuary it had provided.

\*\*\*

John startled awake to the insistent ringing of his hotel phone. He fumbled for it, noting that it was just past 6 am. It was Rosaria.

"John!" She sounded breathless and agitated. "I'm sorry to wake you, but there has been a terrible accident at St. Agatha's. The roadway above the catacombs has collapsed and two people are believed to be trapped below. I'm on my way there and only five minutes away from your hotel. Can you be ready? I knew you'd want to be there. I haven't been able to contact Victor yet, but I'll pick you up at the front of the hotel as soon as you're ready."

"Oh my God!" John exclaimed, clambering out of bed and hastily slipping on some clothes. *Victor,* he prayed, *Victor, please be alright.* He was waiting at the front entrance as Rosaria drove up.

"I hardly know anything yet, though I'm covering the story," she spoke rapidly. "I had a call from Sergeant Caruana at the police department. He said that a rescue team was on the way. He too is related – most of us here on the island are. We've both tried to call Victor, but there has been no reply!"

## In the Image of His God

As they entered the square in front of St. Paul's Church, they ran into the familiar yellow tape used to blockade a crime or accident scene. Rosaria parked the car and approached the duty police officer. He recognized her immediately and waved them both through. They ran down the narrow one-way Triq Hal Bajjada toward the monastery entrance. Halfway there, they found Sergeant Caruana crouched over a gaping hole in the road. Spotlights were hastily being rigged to add to the slowly increasing daylight that was beginning to filter into the darkness below.

"What can you tell us, Raymond?" Rosaria asked Sergeant Caruana.

"Not a lot at this stage, I'm afraid. I have just got here myself. There appear to be two people trapped in the debris below. The paramedics are down there now."

"I'm afraid one's gone," a voice from below called up. "He seems to be a novice priest. We're trying to remove the large slab that apparently crushed him. The other is a priest, judging by his robes. He seems to be alive, but unconscious. He's pinned beneath a support beam that appears to have collapsed."

Rosaria grabbed John's arm. "It must be Victor!" she cried.

John had already come to that conclusion. Knowing the catacombs as he did, he knew that only Victor had access to the area beneath the street where the catacombs had collapsed. "Can you get us permission to go down there?" he asked urgently.

"Raymond!" Rosaria called out. "We believe the priest is my uncle, Father Victor. This is Dr. Peters, a close friend of his and one of the archaeologists responsible for excavating the catacombs. He feels we may be able to help. We'll both be able to identify Victor, if it is him."

"Hang on a minute and I'll check with the paras. It's their call, I'm afraid."

Sergeant Caruana moved to a command post that had been set up beside the gaping hole in the road, returning almost immediately with the news that they could go below, but under strict orders that they were to stay out of the way and follow any instructions the rescue officers gave them. They both agreed immediately.

"I must insist on these," Sergeant Caruana said, handing them both hard hats. "And be careful down there. We don't want any more victims."

They both instantly recognized Victor's ashen face. His eyes were closed and there were no visible signs of life. He lay pinned beneath a large beam that had been the main support for the roof beneath the roadway.

"I warned him about that support structure just the other day," John whispered to Rosaria.

John glanced around in the dim light, part spotlight and part breaking daylight. He immediately caught sight of the crumpled pillowcase lying at the mouth of the canopy tomb. All eyes were on the efforts to free Victor. John slid back along the narrow catacomb passage and with his foot nudged the pillowcase-wrapped object inside the tomb and out of sight. Now was not the time to reveal the contents – if it was, in fact, what John hoped it might be. Even Rosaria had not noticed John's move in the limited light and the tense atmosphere that prevailed.

There were now four rescuers attempting to lift the heavy beam from off Father Victor. The sergeant in charge called out to John and Rosaria.

"Could you try to slide the priest clear if we lift the beam?" he yelled.

"Of course!" John shouted back.

With Rosaria's help, he eased Victor out from under the massive beam of wood.

"Don't lift him," a paramedic called, rushing over as soon as the beam had been lowered to the ground. "We'll take it from here."

Rosaria thought she saw a flicker of movement on Victor's eyelids as the paramedic applied an oxygen mask to his face.

"Okay," he called up to those above, "lower the gurney, please."

Ten minutes later, Victor was being placed in a waiting ambulance for transport to the hospital. Rosaria was allowed to travel with him. John would follow in her car.

Though still unable to speak, Victor had regained consciousness by the time they arrived at St. Luke's. Rosaria had held the priest's hand throughout the twenty-five-minute ride. He was rushed straight to the emergency ward and Rosaria went in search of John. He had managed to find parking space and was entering the main building when Rosaria caught up with him. Together they returned to the emergency ward to await news.

As they sat together, John explained to Rosaria what he believed had happened and what he had done with what he believed was the missing casket.

"My guess," he told her, "is that Victor caught the young novice – I believe it will turn out to be Brother Darren – with the casket and they had a struggle, resulting in the dislodgement of the support beams. I can think of no other scenario that would fit the circumstances, if indeed the pillowcase does contain the casket. I didn't want to say anything while we were there, as the casket may have been considered evidence and confiscated by the police. I know that's the last thing Victor would want."

Rosaria looked puzzled. "But I don't understand why Victor wouldn't want the police to know he had recovered the casket. They knew it had been stolen."

John wished he could explain to her that the contents were not actually what they were supposed to be.

"I'm sure Victor will advise them of the casket's return at the appropriate time," he reassured her. "Trust me. In light of my conversations with him over the last few days, I think it's best left to him."

John was saved by the arrival of the duty doctor. He obviously recognized Rosaria and after an acknowledging handshake told her that her uncle was going to be alright. "He has been severely traumatized by the whole experience and we thought it best to sedate him, but –"

"Is he badly hurt?" John broke in.

"Well, there is severe muscle trauma and the x-rays show a couple of broken bones, but, on the whole, he's been very lucky."

"But we saw him pinned to the ground under that beam!" Rosaria cried.

"Yes, but apparently he escaped the full weight of the beam. You see, it had wedged against the side of the catacomb. Nothing short of a miracle!"

"Thank God!" John said. "How long do you think he'll be hospitalized?"

"A few days, I expect. We'll have a better idea when we've completed the tests tomorrow." Patting Rosaria's shoulder, he continued, "You both look like you could do with some rest. I suggest you call or come back later today. By then he should be sufficiently recovered to talk to you."

Watching Sergeant Caruana approaching them, he added, "I'm sure the police have questions, but we aren't allowing any officers near the patient until he has recovered fully."

Sergeant Caruana reached them just as the doctor left, giving them a reassuring nod.

"Thank God he's okay," Raymond sighed, as he too embraced Rosaria. "I guess you know the deceased is Victor's young novice, Brother Darren."

"Yes, that's what we figured," she said.

"They must have been working together when the beam collapsed. A tragic accident. We've contacted Darren's parents – they are no longer living together, but his father is on his way here to identify the body." He paused. "We'll be able to get a full statement from Father Victor in a couple of days, I'm sure."

John turned to Raymond. "I was working with Father Victor in the '50s when we originally excavated the area that collapsed. Would you have any objection if I visit the site and see if I can shed any light on just what might have caused the collapse?"

"I'm sure our people would be more than happy to hear anything you might be able to contribute to the investigation. I'll notify our local people at the site to give you unrestricted access," Raymond said.

# Chapter 17
(Day 5: midmorning)

Rosaria left to file her story and John returned to his hotel to find Father Victor's package awaiting him. Over a quick cup of coffee, he read Victor's letter and marveled at the two enclosures, particularly the original Da Vinci letter. He would have given a lot to examine it more thoroughly, but he had no time to spare.

Locking the package in his briefcase and resetting the combination lock, he decided he had to act quickly. He first had to return to the catacombs and check out the contents of the pillowcase before anyone else discovered it. He also wished to make sure that there was nothing incriminating in Brother Darren's room that might refer to the silver casket. His family would obviously take possession of all his personal items almost immediately.

John changed into fresh clothes and headed for the reception desk. At the last minute, he thought to take the wheel-along carry case that usually housed his photographic equipment and laptop. The casket should fit nicely in there if, in fact, that's what the pillowcase contained.

John caught a taxi to Rabat and had no problem gaining access. The officer in charge had already heard from Sergeant Caruana and was expecting him – though not quite so soon.

"Let me know if you need anything," the duty officer told John. "By the way what's in the case?" he asked.

"Just my photographic equipment," he told the officer, who seemed satisfied with the answer.

"Our photographers have just left. I'm sure you know what you're doing. Raymond says you were one of the original archaeologists, is that correct?"

"Yes," replied John, "but that was fifty years ago," he chuckled, as he made his way down the emergency ladder the police had put in place.

The emergency spotlight brightly illuminated the mass of rubble and wood that still blocked the passageway. John climbed over and made his way to the entrance of the canopy grave. He was completely alone. He reached in and withdrew the pillowslip. Whatever was inside was not light. He instinctively knew it was the casket. Carefully, he withdrew the precious object. The papal seals were still intact. He slid the casket back into the pillowcase and hastily opened his case, relieved to find the silver casket fit inside perfectly. It was late afternoon and John knew the inhabitants of St. Agatha's would be at afternoon prayers. He headed back down the catacombs to the crypt and into the main building. Hopefully, he could get to Victor's room without being challenged.

He was in luck. The passages were still deserted. He quickly entered Victor's room and hid the silver casket under the bed. He felt sure no one would be searching Victor's room! On John's first visit, Victor had pointed out Darren's room opposite his own. John hurried across the hall. There were no locks on any of the novice's doors. Quietly, he opened Darren's door and entered, closing it softly behind him. The room was very neat and sparsely furnished, though he noticed that the bed was unmade. A diary lay on the bedside table. John slipped it into his pocket. There seemed little else other than a few personal mementos.

Just as he was about to leave, he noticed something sticking out from under Darren's pillow. Darren had obviously used his own pillowcase to wrap the casket, but as John looked closely he noticed an envelope. It bore the seal of the Illuminati – the Great Pyramid of Cheops, with the missing capstone replaced by an eye, the 'All-Seeing Eye'! John thrust the bulging envelope into his breast pocket and headed back toward the crypt and the secret passageway.

"I was getting worried," the duty officer remarked, as John emerged from below. "I called down a few times and got no reply."

"Sorry about that." John smiled sheepishly. "It's been so long since I worked here, I just had to take the opportunity to re-visit the crypt and offer a few words of prayer for Father Victor."

"I'm sure he would thank you for that. Is there anything else you need?"

"No, thank you. I'll head back to my hotel and review the pictures and my notes," he replied. "Please thank Sergeant Caruana for me. I'll be in touch."

John's cab was waiting and he soon found himself back in his room at the Radisson. He heaved a sigh of relief. He couldn't have hoped for a better result from his mission. The casket was safely in Victor's room and, as far as he could find, there was nothing to connect Darren with the dreaded Illuminati. John remembered the envelope he'd placed in his breast pocket. Removing it, he examined the sealed envelope. Knowing he had no other choice, he carefully prised it open. It contained a wad of 100-lira notes. John counted 100. 10,000 lire! No wonder the young man had been tempted. John decided to leave the matter to Victor. He took the envelope and the two priceless letters he had locked in his briefcase and deposited them in his safety deposit box at the hotel.

He would call Rosaria and arrange to meet her at the hospital later that evening – right now, he needed some rest. He fell asleep almost as soon as his head hit the pillow.

It was almost 6.45 pm when John awoke. He reached for the phone and called Rosaria.

"Any news?" he asked.

"I've been waiting for your call," she said. "Victor is going to be fine. He's 'resting comfortably' as they say, and the doctor said it was best to let him sleep. He has a couple of broken bones, but other than that he should be okay." John heard the relief in her voice.

"I'm sure you could do with a good night's sleep as well," she laughed.

John wanted so much to share with her what he had accomplished, but that could wait. He agreed he was tired.

"I think I'll have a quick bite and hit the sack," he said. "Shall we meet at the hospital in the morning?"

"Let's say 10 am. Would that be okay with you?"

"Sounds fine," John agreed. He wanted to get there before her, as there was much that he needed to discuss with Victor in private. He would try to get there half an hour before she arrived. "Goodnight and thanks for the good news."

Deep in thought, John made two phone calls. The first was to Father Muscat. The second was to the airline office. He was due to fly out the following evening after completing his work with the Rabat Shroud, but needed to spend at least a few more days on the island. He knew that Victor would have to find a safeguard to prevent a similar situation from recurring. A plot was developing in the back of his mind, but he would first need Victor's blessing.

He didn't change, but went straight down to the hotel restaurant for dinner. He ordered rack of lamb, one of his favorites, and followed it with a banana split, another of his weaknesses. John had a sweet tooth, there was no mistake – *and this time I deserve my dessert!* he joked to himself.

After dinner, he decided to take a short stroll around the hotel grounds and enjoy the evening view across the bay. The boats bobbed rhythmically on the calm waters and the lights were slowly being switched on, creating delightful patterns across the water. For the first time since his return to Malta, he felt at ease and at home back here. The convention had been an outstanding success and he had been invited to speak at next year's gathering, though the destination was yet to be decided. The Shroud was, John felt, secure, at least for the moment.

As he walked on, taking deep gulps of the sea air, he wondered if Victor would agree to his proposed solution. He had already got Father Muscat, the curator of the Wignacourt Museum, to permit him to restore the frame on the Shroud of Rabat and give it a more prominent position in the museum. This was part of the reason he had extended his stay for another week. The thought that he would be able to spend more time with Rosaria, whose company he was beginning to enjoy more than he knew he should, suddenly crossed his mind.

He returned to his room and settled into bed, going over the events of this remarkable day. Before he knew it, his eyelids drooped shut and he was soon sound asleep.

## Chapter 18
### (Day 6: morning)

John arrived at the hospital just after 9 am. He had taken the precaution of calling the hospital before leaving his hotel, to make sure Victor was awake and was allowed visitors. The duty nurse assured him that Victor was alert and looking forward to John's visit. He had had no other visitors, the nurse informed him.

Wanting to get to Victor before the police and Rosaria, he hastily made his way to Victor's room. Though Victor had been at the hospital for just over a day, the room was filled with flowers. Victor slowly pushed himself up as John approached.

"Easy, now," John warned him, sitting down at his friend's bedside and easing him down. "Just lie back down, Victor, and tell me what happened. If you feel up to it, that is."

Victor immediately launched into a full account of the previous night's happenings. He explained how he had confronted Darren, who he believed was holding the silver casket wrapped in a pillowcase. Clutching John's hand, he described how they had struggled and fallen against the loose upright support. Victor remembered snatching the pillowcase and seeing it rolling away as he felt the crash of the overhead collapse and lost consciousness.

"Thank God you're all right!" John exclaimed. "Rosaria and I were worried to death that you might not survive the massive subsidence. We guessed it was both you and Darren who were trapped. I suppose they've told you that Darren didn't make it?" John asked.

Victor closed his eyes as if praying. "Yes," he sighed. "It was my first question when I regained consciousness. It's so sad. Despite his shortcomings, I was truly growing to love the boy. He'd had a troubled upbringing, came from a broken home, I believe, and was open to temptation …"

He leaned closer to John and lowered his voice to a whisper, even though they were alone in the room. "John, I believe the Illuminati were behind the plot to steal the Shroud." He recounted what he had overheard from outside Darren's room. "Perhaps if I'd done something then, young Darren would still be alive. But it was all such a shock. I felt it best to wait till morning to challenge him. It was more by chance than design that I followed him to the secret passage."

Noticing Victor's deep anxiety, John interrupted his story. "Victor, you did the right thing. There's no way you can blame yourself for what happened. Besides, there are things we must discuss before anyone else arrives."

John watched the old priest nod in agreement. "First, I don't believe anything will be achieved by telling the police the whole story. They've already assumed that the whole incident was nothing more than an unfortunate accident. I would simply tell them that you were both attempting to fix the loose upright when the whole thing collapsed," John suggested. "Further, to completely ease your mind, I've taken care of the casket."

Watching Victor's eyes widen in amazement, he continued, "I've placed it under your bed at St. Agatha's. I don't believe anyone will go into your room until you return. The seal is still unbroken, you'll be glad to hear." John noticed the relief that flooded Victor's face.

"Thank you, John. I have no idea how you accomplished that, but you have my undying thanks for your help."

"There's more," John said somberly. "I took the precaution of searching Darren's room in case there were any tell-tale documents or notes that might mention the casket. There were none. However, I did discover 10,000 lire under his pillow. It must have been the pay-off! I've placed it securely in the safety deposit box at the hotel to await your instructions."

Victor absorbed the information, nodding slowly in understanding. "We need," John continued, "a good cover story as to how you found the missing casket. I suggest we don't mention it until you're released from here. Nobody outside Rosaria and myself know that this whole affair had anything to do with the missing object."

"I believe you're right, John." Victor smiled thankfully. "You know, you haven't changed a bit. I knew I could rely on you to solve this whole mess. I can't imagine the problems I would have created if left to my own devices throughout this whole horrifying experience." The priest blinked back tears as he grasped John's hand in his.

"Victor, my dear friend, It is *I* who should be thanking *you*. You have given me the opportunity of a lifetime, to play an active role in the history and preservation of Christendom's most holy relic. For that, I can never thank you enough," John said sincerely.

"While we're alone, let me tell you what I have in mind. There is much to be done before I leave."

John pulled up a chair and began to unfold his somewhat crazy idea for the preservation of the precious icon. It was an idea that had popped into his mind while he had been discussing the restoration of the frame of the Rabat Shroud with Father Muscat.

"I believe, Victor, that if the Shroud continues to be housed in the casket in the relatively unsecured crypt, the holy relic is, at the very least, highly vulnerable and there is every possibility that there may be another attempt to steal it," John said. "As good-intentioned as the Pope's idea was, he could not have been aware that there was obviously a leak in his internal security. Some person from those he trusted with the secret must have known of the switch and informed the Illuminati. You cannot take the chance that they will simply give up their quest just because Brother Darren met his end."

Victor, deep in thought, nodded in agreement.

"What if, unbeknown to even the Pope, we were to again switch the cloths?"

"What do you mean?" Victor gasped.

"The Holy Shroud of Rabat," John said with a smile. Meeting Victor's uncomprehending look, he explained further. "As I believe I told you, they have agreed that I can restore the frame on the Rabat Shroud and reposition it in a more prominent and secure position within the Wignacourt Museum. The cost is to be met by the Society in lieu of a fee for my appearance at their convention."

"But weren't you supposed to be working on that today? You said you were returning to Las Vegas this evening," Victor commented.

"I've managed to reschedule my flight and rearrange things with Father Muscat. I need more time here to put my plan into action. If you agree, that is."

"What is the plan, John? You said something about a switch…"

John's face betrayed his excitement. Even though they were alone in the room, he bent closer to Victor and lowered his voice.

"What if we switch the genuine article for the Rabat copy and place the Rabat Shroud in the silver casket? It's unlikely that anyone would attempt to steal the Rabat copy, as there are so many of copies of the Shroud in Europe. I intend to encase it in a specially designed display case high on the wall of a room that the museum is making available for the project. Security cameras would monitor it twenty-four hours a day, and the special case I am having flown in would protect it from fading and any possible vandalism. What do you think?" John asked eagerly.

Victor had listened intently to his old friend's proposal. To say he was dumbstruck at the idea of not only going against His Holiness's instructions, but also taking such a monumental risk without the Vatican's approval would have been an understatement!

Before he could comment, they were interrupted by the arrival of Rosaria and Sergeant Caruana.

John greeted Rosaria with a hug and shook hands with Raymond. Rosaria hugged her uncle, her eyes suspiciously bright.

"Oh Victor!" she said tearfully. "Thank God you are alright!"

"Just a broken bone or two," Victor told her, raising his left arm above the covers.

For the first time, John noticed the cast on his friend's arm.

"I'll be fine in a few days," Victor smiled, reaching out to shake Raymond's outstretched hand.

"Are you feeling up to talking for a few minutes?" Raymond asked. "I'd like to get the official paperwork out of the way. There will, of course, be an inquest in light of young Brother Darren's demise."

"Certainly Raymond. It was all very simple, really," Victor said, glancing at John. "Brother Darren and I had both arisen early. We were trying to secure the support beam that had, over the years, become somewhat shaky with all the traffic overhead, and suddenly the whole structure collapsed. That's the last thing I remember before I awoke in the ambulance and Rosaria explained what had obviously happened to dear Darren. God rest his soul."

"That's what we assumed," Raymond replied. "A true tragedy – no question. I'll file my report and advise you when the inquest is to take place. We'll need you to appear, provided that you're fully recovered, of course."

"I'm sure I'll be fine. I believe Darren's parents are coming to see me this afternoon. Father Tomlin, St. Agatha's head priest, is bringing them, I've been told. I understand he was here most of the night, even though I wasn't allowed visitors."

"Thank you Victor, I'll leave you to your guests and will see you all again shortly, I'm sure." Turning to Rosaria and John, he said, "Thank you both for your help."

Rosaria chatted away to Victor, unaware that he was absorbing very little of her conversation. His mind was still trying to come to grips with John's seemingly outlandish proposal.

After about twenty minutes, the doctor bustled in and suggested that Victor get some rest before another series of tests. John arranged to return later that day.

"Give my idea some thought, Victor," he said, as he and Rosaria were leaving.

"I can assure you I will be thinking of nothing else, John. See you about 4 pm."

John and Rosaria parted at the entrance to St. Luke's after arranging to meet for dinner. John was off to the Wignacourt Museum to discuss the Rabat Shroud restoration with Father Muscat. There was much to do. He couldn't help but wonder what poor Victor had made of his proposal. Hopefully, he would have an answer that afternoon.

John's thoughts drifted to the 10,000 lire he had removed from Darren's room. He wanted to give the money to Darren's parents, but that presented two problems. For one, he was not sure that was what Darren would have wanted. For another, he wondered where he could tell them the money came from. Obviously another problem for Victor to solve!

Another crazy idea entered his head. What about an anonymous donation to set up a trust for the preservation of the Shroud of Rabat in memory of Brother Darren? The more he thought about it, the better it sounded. How ironic if the funds paid by the Illuminati ended up protecting the very object they intended to take into their possession! John laughed out loud as he pulled into a parking space opposite the museum.

Father Muscat was waiting for him in his office, which was located just inside the entrance, at the top of the stairway leading to St. Paul's grotto. Father Victor's present condition took up the first five minutes of their conversation.

They walked to the small room that currently housed the Shroud of Rabat. The museum was desperately short of funds and it was a struggle to maintain the collection of magnificent artifacts that were entrusted to its care. The room contained a full size photographic copy of the image on the Shroud taken by the STURP team during the investigative study some years earlier. It stood upright in a corner facing the Rabat Shroud, which hung on the northern wall in an old frame – the original frame, John deduced – at knee level. A small plaque beside it gave the date as 1663. It received little attention from visitors, displayed so unceremoniously in this small, dimly lit room. John intended to change all that.

He and Father Muscat discussed closing the room while it was being re-painted and the new display case that John had ordered from Italy installed. It was to be mounted high on the north wall, tilted down like a giant flat screen TV, well out of reach of any visitors, but in full view of all below. Special lighting would also be installed and, most important, a CCTV camera with a recording device that operated 24/7.

The case would be automatically illuminated when visitors entered the room and would stay illuminated for only three minutes at a time. Similar lighting had been installed at the Hypogeum in Tarxien, which dated back to 4,000 years before Christ and was listed as a World Heritage Treasure.

John assured Father Muscat that he would do most of the work on the display himself and at the very least he would be in attendance at all times while the work was being carried out. John requested a key and exclusive access to the area during the restoration. Father Muscat readily agreed. As a security precaution, John would arrange to have the lock fitted himself so that he had the only key.

That settled, Father Muscat asked, "And have you heard anything lately about the missing silver casket with St. Paul's letters?"

The question surprised John, though he knew that Father Muscat was fully aware that the casket had been missing. After all, it was in his jurisdiction. The grotto was the responsibility of the Wignacourt administration.

"It's strange you should ask," John told him. "Father Victor has discovered that one of the novice monks, Brother Darren, had removed the casket for cleaning and had omitted to inform anyone. He was terrified about his lapse of duty when he realized the casket had been reported stolen and couldn't work up the nerve to confess to Victor till yesterday. It will be back in place at the foot of St. Paul as soon as Victor is released from hospital. Brother Darren is the one who was working with Victor in the catacomb beneath the road when it collapsed. Unfortunately, Darren didn't make it."

"Yes, I met Brother Darren on several occasions. It's a tragic loss. Well, I'll leave you to get on with your work. Let me know if you need anything."

John remained in the small room for several hours, taking measurements and examining the frame in which the ancient cloth had been displayed for so many years. He saw no difficulty in switching the cloths, as this old frame would have to be replaced anyway. That is, if Victor agreed!

He hated to admit it even to himself, but for a brief moment, just before he visited Victor, he had considered making the switch whilst the priest was recovering in hospital and not even telling him! He knew full well how heavily the moral decision regarding his proposal would weigh on the old priest's already weary mind. Both of them knew that, eventually, the Pope would have to be informed!

# Chapter 19
(Day 6: late afternoon)

Victor was sitting propped up in bed when John entered his hospital room.

"How's it going, old friend?" John asked as they embraced, John being careful to avoid jolting Victor's cast.

"Well, I wish you'd give me some kind of warning before you hit me with a proposal like that again!" the old priest laughed. "You put me into a state of shock, I think. It's a good job I wasn't attached to a cardiograph at the time; the needle would've jumped clear off the page!"

They both laughed.

"Seriously though, John, you're quite right. The Shroud in its present location is at great risk. I know the Pontiff's main concern would be the safety of the Shroud and he will have to be informed as soon as possible about what has taken place here. The more I think about your suggested solution, the more I like it. At least until I'm able to meet with His Holiness myself and explain what has happened. It is

## In the Image of His God

obvious he is not aware that the location of this most sacred relic is known to the Illuminati. Nor that there is obviously a leak in his internal security."

Victor sat up straighter, leaning back against the pillows. "What exactly would you need to pull this off?" he asked.

"Well, I've just spent the afternoon at the Wignacourt and everything is in place for me to get started on the re-display of the Rabat Shroud."

Recalling the discussion, he added, "By the way, Father Muscat asked if there were any news about the missing casket. I took the liberty, Victor, of making up a story on the spot. Again, I hope you don't mind. I told him that Darren had removed the silver casket to clean it, had omitted to tell anyone, and only confessed to you yesterday. I said you'd be returning it to the foot of St. Paul as soon as you were released from the hospital."

Watching Victor digest this information, he went on, "At present, the silver casket is in your room, so I would need access and somewhere secure to exchange the contents. It will take a day or two to get the room at the museum ready, and the display cabinet I have ordered is being flown in tomorrow."

"That was clever thinking," Victor remarked. "There's a small workshop behind the altar in the crypt. Do you remember, we set it up all those years ago? It has been little used since. Now it just houses some materials used to preserve the frescoes and a few cleaning supplies. I could arrange with Father Tomlin for you to have exclusive access, as well as the use of my room. You would have complete privacy and, I believe, enough room to work."

"Great, Victor! I'd forgotten all about that room. We used it to clean up the artifacts and pottery fragments that we unearthed, if I remember correctly."

"That's the one," Victor said. "It would be ideal for your purpose."

"By the way, Raymond rang me this afternoon and asked if I would oversee the repairs to the road so as not to damage the catacombs below. Of course I agreed."

"I'm not surprised," Victor chortled. "Because our catacombs are owned by St. Agatha's, very few of the government archaeologists have ever visited the complex. Their focus has been on the catacombs at St. Paul's opposite. They are probably glad you're here!"

"Okay, then, it's agreed. I'll start arrangements if you'll take care of Father Tomlin for me."

"I'll call him now," Victor said. "He only left here a couple of hours ago, with Darren's parents. Very sad. I'm afraid I told a little white lie and said that their son had possibly saved my life by taking the main weight of the falling debris. There is little to be gained in telling the truth. Let God be his judge."

Something else suddenly occurred to him. "What do you suggest we do with the money?" he asked John.

"Well, you did ask me to prepare you for any further crazy ideas I might come up with, so get ready!" John grinned.

He told Victor about his idea of an anonymous donation for a restoration trust in Brother Darren's memory.

"Well I'll be!" Victor exclaimed. "Now I've heard it all. The man steals the casket, for all intents and purpose is a member of the Illuminati, is the cause of my near death – and we are going to set up a restoration trust in his memory!"

They both burst into uncontrollable laughter.

"I truly don't know how you come up with these ideas, John. Perhaps I've been closeted for too long. I think that's a great idea. How ironic!"

# In the Image of His God

John waited while Victor rang Father Tomlin at St. Agatha's.

"Okay," he said, after hanging up. "We're all set. Father Tomlin is expecting you to call by at 9 am tomorrow to get the keys. I guess it's all in your hands now, John." Victor squeezed John's hand lovingly as the two parted. John headed for a quiet dinner with Rosaria and, hopefully, an early night.

There was little doubt that the affection and respect John and Rosaria had developed for each other in the few days they had been thrown together was mutual. Again, John wondered, *What I would have given to have met her twenty years ago or even been twenty years younger now!*

They had decided to go Japanese tonight. Not far from St. Julian's, where John's hotel was situated, was the tourist district of Sliema and the Japanese restaurant in the Fortuna Resort Hotel – one of Rosaria's favorite eating-places. John thought of his visits to the Hamada Restaurant in Las Vegas. The antics of the Asian chefs as they prepared his beef, shrimp, chicken and fried rice before his very eyes never ceased to entertain him. He truly enjoyed going there and hoped this place would be comparable.

Rosaria looked wonderful dressed in a simple black strapless cocktail dress that emphasized her lovely figure. She reminded him of the statues of Nefertiti that he had marveled at as a young man studying for his degree in archaeology.

He recalled a poem he had read and always remembered, written during the New Kingdom era. He shared it with Rosaria.

"She looks like the morning rising star,

At the start of a happy year,

Shining bright, fair of skin,

Lovely the look of her eyes,

Sweet the speech of her lips...

With graceful steps she treads the ground,

Captures my heart by her movements,

She causes all men's necks

To turn about to see her;

Joy has he whom she embraces,

He is like the first of men."

"That's beautiful!" she sighed, her eyes sparkling with delight. "You must write it out for me."

They opted for the tappenyaki dinner – soup, tender beef fillets, steamed rice and green tea ice cream – along with a platter of sushi. After complementing the chef, John shared one of his Vegas chef's tricks with him: an onion sliced in the shape of a pyramid, filled with brandy and ignited, shot flames and smoke into the air like a volcano.

The rest of their conversation was mostly about Victor. Rosaria was, of course, still unaware of the true contents of the silver casket. John told her the story he had given Father Muscat about the disappearance of the silver casket and that Victor would return it on his release from the hospital. He also told her about their idea of the trust in Brother Darren's name. She found it as ironic and amusing as had Victor. She agreed that the truth would achieve little and cause a great deal of pain to many who had tried so hard to help the young man find his real calling in life. It was they, not Brother Darren, who would suffer the pain. She promised to write a nice piece about the mystery donor and the purpose of the restoration trust.

"If," she added, smiling impishly, "you promise to write out that lovely poem for me."

She dropped John at his hotel. "I know you'll be busy tomorrow, and I have some catching up to do as well. Give me a call before you visit Victor. I'll make sure I get there as well."

"I'll do that."

He watched her drive away, already looking forward to seeing her again.

# Chapter 20
(Day 7: morning)

John woke early the following day and drove straight to St. Agatha's after a light breakfast.

Father Tomlin was waiting for him at the entrance. Together, they entered the crypt leading to the catacombs. The iron gate to the left of the altar led to the section of the labyrinth of passages that was not open to the public and to the secret passage leading to St. Paul's grotto. Immediately inside was a steel doorway that was hardly visible in the poor light. The doorway opened into a small workshop that had obviously not been used for some time.

It immediately brought back a flood of memories for John.

"It's been a few years since I've been down here," Father Tomlin remarked. "I don't believe I've ever entered this room."

He smiled as he turned to John. "I'll get one of the novices to clean it out for you, Dr. Peters. It will be ready for you this afternoon. When do you intend to start work?"

## In the Image of His God

"They're delivering the new showcase for the Rabat Shroud this afternoon and, with your permission, I'll have them deliver it here rather than to the Wignacourt. I'd be grateful if you could assign someone to carry the existing frame with the Shroud from the Wignacourt Museum to this place later today. Its not heavy, just a bit awkward for me to manage."

"That would be no problem," Father Tomlin said. "Would about 3.30 be okay?"

"I'm sure that'd be fine. I'll check with Father Muscat and get back to you only if there is a problem."

"Is the lighting here adequate? I can get additional lights set up if you require them."

"That would be excellent," John replied gratefully. "Father Victor suggested that I could use his room as my office for the few days he will be in hospital. If I may, I'll get organized there now ..."

"Yes, he told me about that, though I'm sure we can find you more suitable accommodation to work in. Father Victor's room is very small. Are you sure you'll be alright using that?"

"Absolutely," John was quick to reply. "I simply need somewhere to crash in the afternoons for a few hours and the use of Victor's computer."

"Very well, then, if you're sure you'll be alright. I'll keep the keys to this room until this afternoon, by which time we'll have it cleaned up and the lights installed. Will you be here at 3.30 to supervise the moving of the frame?"

"My plans are to be here for the rest of the day. I'll be in Victor's room if you should need me. If I'm not there, I'll be supervising the repairs to the roof of the catacombs. They start the repairs this morning, I hear?"

"I believe so; the crews arrived about an hour ago." Father Tomlin led the way back towards the monastery building and Father Victor's room. "I'll leave you to your own devices," he smiled. "If you need anything, just call me. You have my extension, I believe?"

"Thank you, Father. You've been most kind."

John closed the door and slipped the bolt. Priests, unlike novices, could lock their rooms from the inside. This was important, as John did not want to be disturbed when he removed the papal seal and the precious contents of the silver casket.

John immediately strode to the bed and reached under it, feeling for the pillowcase-wrapped casket. To his relief, it was exactly where he had hidden it the previous day.

Clearing an area on Victor's desk, he placed the casket before him. For John this was the greatest moment of his life. Only the Pope's seal stood between him and the greatest relic of all time – the blood-stained cloth that had wrapped the torn and battered body of Christ himself just before his resurrection! A cloth that contained the only actual image of Jesus known to man! Though it had been some time since John had knelt in prayer, he dropped to his knees, bowed his head and thanked God for giving him this remarkable opportunity.

John reverently examined the seal. The crossed keys of gold and silver, bound with a red cord, he knew, symbolized the keys to the Kingdom of Heaven. The Triple Crown or tiara represented the Pope's three functions as supreme priest, supreme pastor and supreme teacher. The gold cross on a globe surmounting the tiara was meant to symbolize the sovereignty of Jesus.

Cautiously, John examined the manner in which the seal had been applied. It was attached to a gold ribbon that passed through the clasp of the casket. It was obviously not intended to be a securing device, but more a symbol of the authority and the ultimate protection of the Vatican. John saw no difficulty in removing and eventually replacing the ribbon with little chance of his unauthorized entry being discovered.

He would need scissors and a strong fabric glue to complete his task. Victor's desk proved a treasure trove of suitable implements and substances. In the topmost drawer, John found a small, sharp pair of surgical scissors and some super glue.

He carefully cut the ribbon at the point nearest the seal. The re-join would be concealed by the seal itself. His hand shaking only slightly in nervous excitement, he gently placed the seal in Victor's desk drawer. Now for the moment of truth. He was tempted to shout, "... and we will open the case, right after these messages from our sponsors!"

For a few short moments, he just sat staring at the silver casket, almost afraid to reach out and lift the now freed latch that was the only thing standing between him and the most holy relic in the world. For some strange reason, an image of Howard Carter, standing at the entrance of King Tutankhamun's tomb flashed into his mind.

*"What can you see?" the voice of Lord Carnarvon asked.*

*"Wonderful things!" Howard replied.*

John shook his head and returned to reality.

Taking a slow, deep breath, he cautiously raised the lid, almost expecting the Mormon Tabernacle Choir to burst into the Ava Maria.

The Shroud was wrapped in a gold satin cloth, tied with a gold ribbon. John carefully undid the bow and removed the outer wrapping just sufficiently to allow him to see the treasure it contained. He had no intention of opening the precious cloth until he was ready to effect the transfer. He gazed in reverent awe at the holy artifact before him. His throat seemed to close up and he felt tears prick his eyes as he thought of the passion of the crucifixion. Slowly, with infinite care, he replaced the gold covering and lowered the lid of the casket. Returning the casket to the pillowcase, he replaced it beneath Father

Victor's bed.

Giving himself a minute or two to regain his breath, John picked up the phone and rang the airport. The new showcase had arrived and would be delivered that afternoon, on schedule. He headed for the catacombs and the site of the cave-in. Work was already underway and new beams were being lowered into the crevice left by the collapsed roadway. John watched as the engineers carefully installed the support beams. Luckily, the collapse was between two large canopy graves, neither of which had been damaged. John slipped through the passageway and made his way to the grotto entrance.

Glancing around him, seeing no one and hearing no sounds, he slid open the rock entrance and proceeded to make his way up to the Wignacourt Museum above. Father Muscat was in his office. The receptionist who normally sat in front of the CCTV monitor was missing, confirming in John's mind that their decision to remove the Shroud from the grotto was a wise one.

"'Morning, Father," John greeted Father Muscat, as he entered his office unannounced. "Sorry to burst in on you, but there was no one outside to announce me."

"Welcome, Dr. Peters. My receptionist just slipped out to get some provisions. What can I do for you?"

"Just confirming that 3.30 is a good time to collect the Rabat Shroud, Father. One of the boys from St. Agatha's is coming over to carry it for me."

"No problem, Dr. Peters. My staff, as few as we are, will be on hand should you need us. I took the liberty of removing the frame from the wall after you left yesterday, in preparation for the move. We're all very excited about the project. It will hopefully give a new lease of life to this tired establishment. Perhaps encourage other projects and provide much-needed funding. The painters are due to start work as soon as you leave this afternoon."

"I know some of the Shroud Society have stayed back especially for the opening; which, if all goes well, we can schedule for the end of the week," John said.

"Well, we're deeply indebted to both you and the Society for your interest in our museum and, of course, the Rabat Shroud. I'm sure 90% of our population has no idea that this replica of the Shroud even exists and has never visited our museum. Hopefully, that will change with the announcement of the new exhibit. We are already preparing a circular for all the schools on the island."

"I can assure you, Father, that we too are appreciative of all the effort you and your dedicated band of followers have put in, with remarkably little funding, to preserve all the treasures in your care, particularly the Rabat Shroud."

The two shook hands and John returned to observing the repair work to the road above the catacombs. The work crews were moving at remarkable speed. The neighborhood had literally been at a standstill since the collapse, as the one-way street was the only access to half of Rabat.

# Chapter 21
(Day 7: midafternoon)

At 3.30 sharp, John answered a knock on the door of Father Victor's room and opened it to see two young schoolboys in St. Agatha's uniform.

"Good afternoon, sir," One of the boys said. "Father Tomlin said you needed some help to move a painting."

"Not exactly a painting, though there are some who would agree with you!" John chuckled. "Yes, thank you for offering your help. We'll head right over to the museum now. I don't want to be too long, as I am expecting a delivery this afternoon."

"We can do it on our own if you like, sir," the other boy suggested.

"I appreciate that," John said. "I would feel much more comfortable if I escorted you, though. Thanks anyway. Shall we go?"

It took them less than half an hour to return to St. Agatha's, despite the turmoil going on in the street connecting the museum to St. Agatha's. It was pedestrian traffic only, for the time being. The two lads left the Shroud on John's newly cleaned workbench in the crypt workshop, just as a truck drew up at the blockade outside. The airport deliverymen carried the new showcase to the crypt workshop and John slipped them five lire for their trouble.

Just about everything he needed to complete his task was now in place. It was 5.30 pm and he had agreed to meet Rosaria at the hospital at 7. He hadn't thought about food all day, but he now started to feel hunger pangs. Was it that or the idea of seeing Rosaria again that caused the fluttering in his stomach?

Food could wait! He needed more private time with Victor before visiting hours at the hospital. On Victor's request, the hospital authorities had allowed John unrestricted access. He made a final inspection of the road repairs before picking up his car in front of the museum and heading off towards St. Luke's.

The crew chief had told him they expected to have the road open the next day if they worked through the night, which they intended to do. Victor would be glad to hear that. All tourist traffic had been halted as a result of the collapse and those funds, as meager as they were, were the only source of income St. Agatha's Crypt and Catacombs enjoyed.

Quite unfairly, John felt, the government-controlled tourist department diverted most of the tourist traffic to St. Paul's Catacombs located opposite St. Agatha's. This despite the fact that the St. Agatha catacombs were in a much better state of preservation and housed some of the most remarkable frescoes on the island. Visitors to St. Paul's were given a recording device and left on their own to explore the catacombs. This lack of supervision had resulted in many visitors covering the walls with unsightly graffiti. All tours to St. Agatha's were accompanied by a guide and, as a result, the place was far better protected from vandals. Not to mention the amazing artifact collection created by Victor at St. Agatha's Museum.

John parked at the hospital and made his way to Victor's room. As usual, his old friend was delighted to see him.

"I almost dread to ask what you've come up with today," Victor said.

Even as they hugged, John was aching to tell his old friend that he had actually laid hands on the Shroud!

"Victor!" John burst out "I've actually touched it!" The emotion of the moment was too much and their eyes swam with tears of joy.

"I can't believe I've actually touched it!"

"Oh, what I would have given to be with you," Victor cried. "All day, my every thought has been of you and the task at hand."

John sat at the old priest's side and recounted the day's events. He told Victor of the seal and the arrival of the new showcase. Victor was delighted to hear that the roadway and the catacomb roof were nearing completion.

"When do you expect to be out of here?" John asked anxiously.

"They tell me, if all goes well I should be able to return to St. Agatha's the day after tomorrow."

"That's fantastic!" John beamed. "I should have everything in place by the end of tomorrow and we could schedule the Rabat Shroud's unveiling for a couple of days later. Rosaria will handle all the publicity and invitations and you'll be there to preside over the event. About thirty or so members of the Shroud Society have remained behind to attend the opening. Rosaria said the President and the Prime Minister would both be sure to attend. If only they knew what they will *really* be looking at!" Both men burst into laughter.

"John, I know I keep repeating myself, but I can never thank you enough!" Victor said again, grasping John's hand.

"Don't be silly, Victor," John replied. "If you had seen me as I opened the casket earlier today, you would realize that it is I who will be indebted to you for the rest of my life!"

He impulsively hugged Victor again. "What's even more precious is the fact that this is a moment in history that will be only shared by the two of us! At least for the time being."

"I must make arrangements to fly to Rome and inform His Holiness as soon as possible," Victor said. "My heart will not rest till I am able to get his blessing on what we have done. I know his only concern will be for the safety of the precious cloth. Perhaps you will accompany me, John? I know he will want to thank you personally."

"My goodness!" John replied. "The thought never crossed my mind. Of course! Needless to say, I would be delighted."

Turning to other matters, John continued, "Rosaria is preparing a press release on the restoration trust in Brother Darren's name for the upkeep of the Shroud exhibit. We've not told anyone as yet and believe you should announce it at the opening ceremony. I know his family will be delighted and so will Father Muscat."

"I'm assuming that you've worked out all the details with Rosaria?" Victor asked, a trifle wryly.

"Yes. Rosaria will claim that the funds were delivered to her anonymously at the *Times Of Malta* office, with a note asking that a trust be established in Brother Darren's honor for some beneficial cause. The note will suggest that you be appointed trustee and therefore you should decide the nature of the trust fund usage. It's unlikely that anyone will query your proposal that the funds be used in the manner we have agreed."

Victor nodded his approval. "It seems you two have thought of everything."

"Well, you have a brilliant niece, Victor. Were I a few years younger, Malta might be in danger of losing one of its sharpest and most beautiful journalists, and I might have gained wife number 6 … or would it be number 7?" John laughed out loud.

"I knew it!" Victor said, shaking his head and smiling affectionately at his friend. "You've got a crush on her, haven't you? 'Rosaria this', 'Rosaria that'… you can't seem to stop talking about her. And do you know something?" He paused meaningfully.

"So, go on, tell me," John said.

"She finds you fascinating. I wonder if there's a little crush on her part as well …"

"I doubt it, flattering as that is. Ah, if only *she'd* been twenty years older …"

"Don't you mean *forty* years older?"

As if on cue, Rosaria entered the room to find both men laughing helplessly at something Victor had obviously just said. Little did she realize that she had been the cause of their evident amusement.

They quickly filled her in on as much as their secret allowed and she agreed to get the initial publicity rolling for the opening of the new Shroud of Rabat exhibit at the Wignacourt Museum. She had a lawyer friend who would set up the trust and have that in place for the opening announcement.

She apologized to John for not being available for dinner that night, as she had to travel to the neighboring Island of Gozo to cover the opening of their new ferry terminal the next day. She would be back in plenty of time to take care of everything and would meet up with John at the Wignacourt Museum the following evening to preview the exhibit with John and possibly Victor, if he could convince the hospital to allow him to leave a few hours ahead of schedule. All being well, John felt, he could have the exhibit up and in place by early evening.

Rosaria kissed them both farewell and headed for the ferry to Gozo. She would spend the night there, rather than face the crossing late at night.

John and Victor went over the final details of their story and the opening procedures before John suggested that he get some take-out Chinese food sent in and they both enjoy dinner right there. Victor was secretly glad not to have to partake of his evening hospital meal, as good as everyone in the kitchen had been. He had quickly become one of their favorites.

The food arrived within forty minutes and they dug into a hearty meal of lemon chicken, sweet and sour pork and special fried rice. Feeling very contented and looking forward to the next day, John drove slowly back to St. Julian's and his bed at the Radisson.

As he passed the Dragonara Casino, he was tempted to indulge in his hometown vice of some slot machine play, but resisted the temptation. Instead, he decided that it might be a fun place to visit on his last evening with Rosaria.

As he settled down for the night, he marveled at what had transpired over the last seven days. From the time he had received the Society's invitation to speak in his beloved Malta and read Father Victor's mysterious letter, it seemed a lifetime had passed. It was as if he had never left the magical island.

Then there was Rosaria! John had thought that romantic emotions were a thing of the distant past. It had been over six years since he had so much as been out on a date. Yet, there was something different about their relationship. It was more platonic than any romantic involvement. He felt he had known her forever. They were so comfortable together, almost as if they were family. John knew he would not forget her in a hurry.

Thinking about her with deep affection, he fell into a deep and relaxing sleep.

# Chapter 22
(Day 8: morning)

As the dawn of the eighth day of his action-packed stay broke over the massive fortifications of the Grand Harbor, John was already heading toward Rabat. He could hardly grasp what had happened in the few short days he had been back on the island. In his wildest dreams, he could never have imagined the events that had unfolded. To think he not only had in his keeping the Holy Shroud, but had actually touched the sacred cloth! It seemed almost as though he were dreaming. He half expected to wake up in his comfortable bed back in hectic Las Vegas at any moment.

John had moved to Las Vegas nearly sixteen years ago. No matter where his frequent travels took him, he was always pleased to be back in the entertainment capital of the world. Las Vegas had changed considerably since his first visit in 1974. John chuckled to himself. Vegas changes almost every day! Literally every month something new opened or was blown up. The city itself had spread its tentacles from mountain to mountain. New housing developments had sprung up in every direction. The beautiful paradise in the desert called Lake Las Vegas was only a short half-hour drive from the bustling world famous strip. With its luxurious Ritz Carlton Hotel and the Casino MonteLago, it conjured up pictures of Italy and was now home to many of the superstars who frequented the city. John spent many a quiet afternoon sitting beside the lake or listening to jazz at a nearby bar.

After parking his car, he made his way directly to Father Victor's room. He would waste little time in transporting the casket to the crypt workshop where he could now keep it under lock and key. He had been insistent that he alone held a key to the small room that was about to become one more of the Shroud's many homes.

No one took any notice of him as, cradling the casket that was once again wrapped in the pillowcase, he made his way to the small room behind St. Agatha's altar. He almost thought the alabaster statue of the saint smiled at him as he passed into the gated passageway and through the padlocked door into the now spotless room.

He placed the pillowcase-wrapped casket on a small stool beside the workbench on which the framed Shroud of Rabat now lay. He wanted to remove the ancient cloth from its equally old frame as carefully as possible. He would re-wrap it in the gold satin that presently encased the actual Shroud and then place it exactly in the same manner as the original inside the silver casket. John felt very strongly that the Shroud of Rabat, though a known reproduction, had still been in contact with the blood of Christ at the time it was laid atop of the original and, as such, deserved all due care and respect that a holy artifact of this rarity deserved.

Anticipating that this would be a slow and painstaking process, John had scheduled the whole day for the task. Hopefully, he would have enough time to also prepare the new showcase for its most sacred occupant. John had decided to wait for Victor before removing the original Shroud from the casket and installing it in its future home. Even though Victor had said nothing, John knew what it would mean to his dear friend to also come in direct contact with this precious icon.

While John worked through the day, Rosaria was busy sending invitations to all the church and government officials and to the President and the First Lady to attend the unveiling of the Shroud of Rabat in its newly refurbished home at the Wignacourt Museum.

By 4 pm the workmen doing the renovation had cleared the room and cleaned up any remaining spots of paint. The room was now a deep crimson, with a gray trim. Fitting colors for the many visitors to reflect on the sacred display that would soon grace its walls! John stuck his head in to check on everything before he headed to the hospital to see Victor. He was pleased with the look. The electricians would install the special lighting and CCTV camera the next morning.

Before heading for St. Luke's, he remembered that Rosaria was attending a press conference that evening. Brian had called him earlier and suggested he have dinner with him and Lola. John looked forward to meeting them again. Although he was pleased with his day's work and anticipated a pleasant evening with Victor as they discussed their plans, he couldn't help feeling a twinge of regret. *Tomorrow will be my last day on the island.*

\*\*\*

Victor had received clearance from the hospital for an early morning release. He would attend mass at St. Agatha's and then join John in the workshop after breakfast. John could feel the excitement emanating from Victor as they discussed John's achievements that day. John described to Victor the new room at the Wignacourt and the equipment that was being installed to ensure security. Victor seemed pleased and more at ease with the plan. After all, he would be the one who had to justify their decision to His Holiness.

"How did you manage to remove the papal seal, John?" Victor asked.

John explained the method used to attach the seal and that he believed that once reattached it would be impossible, without close scrutiny, to detect the fact that the seal had been removed and replaced.

"I believe the seal is designed to signify the Pope's acknowledgement of the contents rather than as a security device," John said, thinking out loud rather than in direct answer to Victor's question.

The two men chatted for over an hour before John departed for his hotel and left Victor to his last night in the hospital.

He was just in time to meet Brian and Lola. He had made a reservation at the Radisson rather than leave the hotel again tonight. He planned an early start tomorrow.

Needless to say, Brian and Lola were both relieved to hear that Victor was recovering and that the casket had been recovered. John explained the cover story that had been given to the authorities to protect the members of the Society from further scrutiny and to preserve Brother Darren's memory. They both agreed with John and Victor's assessment that little would be achieved by pointing a finger at the young novice, all the more so as he was no longer alive to defend his actions, if indeed there was any defense for his removing and concealing the silver casket from it's appointed resting place.

"Who do you think was ultimately responsible, and what prompted him to steal the casket in the first place?" Lola asked John.

"According to a conversation that Father Victor overheard, a group known as the Illuminati were behind the plot to steal the documents contained in the casket," John told them.

In response to their questioning looks, he explained, "The Illuminati are an ancient society, which as far as I can trace, came into being in the late 1700s. This secret society was founded by a Dr. Adam Weishaupt, then professor of canon law at the Bavarian Ingolstadt University. The Order of the Illuminati, as it was known, was a society within the Masonic lodges of Germany. You might say the Illuminati were a secret society within a secret society, though there are many who would disagree!"

"So the origins were German," Lola said. "Didn't it have any opponents back then? I mean, secret societies usually do."

"Records indicate that, in 1785, the Bavarian Government suppressed the movement for plotting to overthrow the Pope and the reigning monarchy of Europe. Since then, there have been accusations that the society, which still exists in some form today, was historically behind the French and American revolutions. There seems to be substantial evidence that they were involved in the spread of communism and even devil worship."

Brian leaned forward. "That's interesting. It means they weren't just powerful, they had friends in high places. What was the motive, would you say?"

"There are many who believe that the Illuminati can be traced back to the Knights Templar and beyond them to the gnostic cults, and even to the early Egyptian societies," John reported. "There seems to be no two scholars who agree on the exact purpose of the group and their present day activities. One thing is certain, however; the ultimate goal of the society is world domination and the destruction of the Catholic Church."

John hesitated briefly before adding, "According to Victor, Brother Darren had been approached by a member of that society and offered a large sum of money for the silver casket and its contents."

"So it would be safe to say that they will possibly still try to get their hands on the casket, despite Brother Darren's untimely death?" Brian asked.

"That, of course, is something we'll have to see, though you're probably right. We must assume that is the case. We're doing everything to tighten security at the grotto as well as the museum."

"That's hardly likely to deter this society if they're as powerful as they seem to be," Lola said thoughtfully.

"Well, it's Father Victor's intention, I believe, to issue a statement that the documents contained in the silver casket have been removed to a secure vault on the instructions of the Pope. However, he's waiting until he has an opportunity to meet with the Pontiff and obtain his approval before any public statement."

The conversation moved on to the subject of magic and illusion and they enjoyed an evening of swapping secrets before John said his goodnights and invited them to attend the opening of the new Shroud of Rabat display at the Wignacourt the next evening. "And you must visit me in Las Vegas when you have an opportunity," he added.

"We can't wait", Brian said, shaking John's hand. "It's long been at the top of our 'bucket list'!"

John dismissed the idea of a short walk and went straight to his room. His message light was flashing when he entered the room and John guessed correctly that it would be Rosaria.

"Just checking to see how your evening went," she said cheerily. "Don't bother to call me back. I'll see you in the morning, as agreed."

John remembered they had agreed to have an early breakfast at his hotel for a quick update on their activities.

# Chapter 23
(Day 9: morning)

As usual, Rosaria arrived promptly and proceeded to fill John in on the arrangements for the opening ceremony and the guest list. She too had a busy day ahead. John told her of his plans to get together with Victor and start work on reframing the Rabat Shroud for its new home. She seemed excited at the job of arranging the unveiling of Malta's sacred cloth, and hosting the event at John's invitation.

"The Prime Minister is not in Malta at present, but I spoke with the President last evening and he said that he would be honored to attend," she told John, her face reflecting her excitement. "His attendance will make sure we have a great media turnout, not to mention a full compliment from the government departments concerned."

John thanked her for all the hours she was putting in. "Victor is so proud of you and your work," he told her. "And I can't believe I'll be leaving this incredible place tomorrow. Could we have dinner together?"

"Of course! I'd love to."

## In the Image of His God

"And I'd love to take you to the Dragonara Palace. I'd thought we'd have a go at the Casino, just for a laugh, and have dinner. What do you think?"

"That'd be wonderful, John. I'll look forward to it."

Knowing that it would be another hour or two before Victor was discharged, John decided to take a different route to Rabat and headed out along the coast road past the village of Bahar ic-Caghaq, where he spotted an ice cream vendor with a stall right on the beachfront. Even at that early hour, John could not resist the temptation to stop and satisfy his craving for something sweet. He ordered a vanilla cup with large black maraschino cherries and demolished it with glee before continuing on to Rabat.

On impulse, he swung left and headed up the hill towards Mosta, where he had lived for a short period during his early years in Malta. The dome of the Mosta church was reputed to be the third largest unsupported dome in the world. John recalled the wartime story of the Italian bomb that fell on the roof of the dome during World War II. The church was packed with worshipers attending early mass when the bomb pierced the roof and lodged there, hanging above their heads. Miraculously, it failed to explode. A replica of the bomb is still displayed in the church for visitors to marvel at today.

John parked for a few minutes, trying to place his old digs, which he remembered being immediately beside the church. He recognized nothing but the church, which leaves an indelible memory on all who visit it. He followed the signs to Rabat and rejoined the familiar road that he seemed to have traveled each day, leading to Rabat and the ancient walled city of M'dina. He parked his car and entered the passageway leading to the crypt at St. Agatha's. Father Victor was waiting patiently at the entrance.

"Good morning, Victor!" John smiled widely. "Sorry I'm a little late. I took a side trip down memory lane."

"I've retrieved the papal seal from my room. I was going to enter the workshop, but they informed me that you have the only key – understandably!" Victor was obviously excited at the prospect of the day's events. "I guess you can understand my excitement at being able to view the cloth at last," he said softly, as they strolled towards the iron gate and John withdrew his key to the small workshop.

"Everything is ready for the transfer, Victor. However, I knew you would want to be present when the Shroud is removed from the silver casket. I've removed the seal but I purposely didn't remove the cloth. Just took a sneak peak," John chuckled. He too was excited at the thought of actually seeing the cloth for the first time.

Together, he and Victor slowly removed the gold satin cloth that wrapped the sacred object and carefully placed the Shroud on the workbench. John was not sure exactly what backing cloth supported the Shroud, though he knew it had recently been changed. The Shroud of Rabat, still mounted in its original frame, now stood beside the new showcase resting against the workshop wall. Clearing the bench top for the holy relic, John had had to improvise on an extension of the workbench, as the cloth was over 14 feet long and 3.7 feet wide.

Glancing at Victor's cast, John frowned. "Why don't you sit this one out? That must be painful."

"Oh, I'm sure it's more a fracture than a break," Victor said dismissively. "It hardly bothers me at all. Let's get started, shall we?"

With extreme caution, they slowly rolled out the precious fabric, marveling at the image as it slowly appeared before them. John felt some of the excitement Secondo Pia must have felt when the image of the face of Jesus first appeared on his photographic plate.

John noted that Victor's hands were shaking visibly as they unrolled the cloth. Tears of wonderment and joy began to fill the old priest's eyes. He was too overcome with emotion to speak. For what seemed an eternity, they both stood motionless, gazing in awe at what now lay before them. Together, they rolled the precious cloth back and placed it to one side.

Although John had spent most of the previous day loosening the ancient frame of the Rabat Shroud, the process of actually removing the Rabat cloth was the most difficult task that lay before them and took them several hours of close and careful work to complete. Finally, having removed it from its frame, they carefully wrapped it in the gold satin cloth that had only a few hours ago held the most sacred relic and placed it carefully in the silver casket. John carefully replaced the papal seal and glued the gold ribbon after passing it through the clasp, ensuring that the joint was invisible and the seal appeared intact.

Together, they managed to lift the new showcase onto the bench, with John taking care to bear most of the weight. It was necessarily large and therefore rather heavy.

John removed the glass front, which had been made from shatterproof glass and specially tinted to preserve the Shroud from even the sophisticated lighting that he had requested. He had majored in museum display preservation and was considered an expert on artifact display techniques.

With extreme care and a strong sense of dedication and commitment for the task they were undertaking, they painstakingly stretched the Shroud into its new home. A feeling of joyous satisfaction overcame them both as they closed the top cover and replaced the glass front. His Holiness would be pleased, Victor felt, with their decision and the work they had undertaken.

They gave the Shroud one more look before they left the room, locking the door behind them. It was time to attend to the rest of the exhibits.

# Chapter 24
(Day 9: evening)

Everything was in place for the big event. John and Victor, Father Muscat and Rosaria had spent most of the day getting the exhibition ready. Victor had placed the silver chest containing the actual Shroud of Rabat in St. Agatha's vault and Rosaria had written an article accompanied by a photograph of Victor locking the silver casket out of harm's way. It would remain there until Victor had a chance to meet with His Holiness.

Father Muscat had shared with John the difficulty he had in maintaining the present museum and its treasured contents and it was partly this that had prompted John to think of the tourist potential and revenue the new Shroud of Rabat exhibit would generate.

The Wignacourt Collegiate Museum is located to the right of St. Paul's Church in Rabat, built above the grotto where it is believed St. Paul spent three months after being shipwrecked on Malta in 60 A.D.. The M'dina promontory, used by the local Bronze Age culture, was transformed into the city of MLT by the Phoenicians and expanded by the Romans to the city of Melite. This Roman town extended from present day M'dina to the area occupied today by St.

## In the Image of His God

Paul's Church. In fact, the church and the straight street in front of it, St. Rita Street, stands on a man-made depression considered to be the Roman ditch of this city. On various occasions, remains of this Roman city had been found, the most noteworthy of which were the remains of the Roman *domus* often erroneously referred to as the Roman Villa. John noted the great job of restoration that the present government's Heritage Department had done on the old villa site.

Though most locals knew of the museum because many school tours were conducted there, few knew of the existence of the hypogeum complex on the ground floor of the Wignacourt Collegiate Museum.

During construction work on the site, the complex was found in the early twentieth century. Sir Themistocles Zammit, who at that time was the museum's director, was called on-site to examine the find, but because of the urgency of the construction works it was reported that he could only partly preserve the tombs. During the Second World War, most of the catacombs were converted to air raid shelters, including the hypogeum at Wignacourt.

At the time of John's archaeological project on the island in the early '50s, many of the late Roman and Byzantine tombs had already been turned into underground chapels, cave dwellings and storage rooms.

There was little doubt in John's mind that the new exhibit would revitalize the museum and bring much-needed tourist lire to Father Muscat's Wignacourt complex.

John and Victor stood alone side-by-side in the now empty refurbished exhibit hall and gazed at their workmanship. Everything had happened so quickly that neither of them had truly had an opportunity to fully comprehend the magnitude of their achievements and to what extent their efforts would contribute to the preservation of Christendom's most sacred relic. Almost instinctively, they turned and embraced each other.

Crowds were already gathering at the sight of the television crews setting up in front of the museum, in anticipation of the arrival of the

President and his wife and official guests. A red carpet had been placed from the sidewalk to the entrance of the main building. Some guests had already started trickling in.

Inside, Father Muscat was hastily making last-minute arrangements and issuing instructions to his staff. Rosaria had the reception area well under control.

Right on schedule, the President's entourage rolled up and was escorted to the main entrance. The guests were served cocktails before following the President and his official party to the new exhibit hall. As they faced the television cameras, John, as the primary benefactor, invited the President to unveil the newly redisplayed Shroud of Rabat.

Cameras flashed and the murmurs in the audience rose to an excited crescendo. The audience fell into a respectful silence as Father Victor took the stand. He offered a brief prayer on behalf of Brother Darren and thanked the benefactor for the funds that made this exhibit financially possible. Next, John made a short speech, thanking Father Victor and Father Muscat for their assistance. On behalf of the Shroud Society, he invited the President to do the honors.

In turn, the President in his speech thanked John for the magnificent restoration job he had done and for bringing this exhibit to public attention.

"I feel sure all of Malta is indebted to both you and the Shroud Society for helping us focus worldwide attention on the unbelievable archaeological sites that abound on our precious island and the unknown treasures that, in many cases, still remain hidden here," the President concluded.

John looked across at Victor and they exchanged smiles. *If only he knew!* John chuckled to himself. *If only they all knew!*

Later, saying their farewells in the privacy of Victor's room, John asked, "You'll stay in touch, won't you, Victor?"

"Of course, my dear friend. I have never been comfortable with email, at least not for personal mail, and I certainly wouldn't trust it to tell you about any… any…"

"…Untoward happenings, shall we say? I'll be thinking of you and the Holy Shroud. And, of course, looking forward to our visit to the Pope."

"And what if I get into trouble and need to contact you? I daren't mention the casket or the Holy Shroud."

"Or even the 'Shroud of Rabat', for that matter. Tell you what, why don't we have a code word?"

"Ah… that takes me back to my schooldays. What do you suggest?"

John pondered awhile, before inspiration struck him. "It would have to be something only you and I would recognize. What about the cave-in where you had such a miraculous escape? It would be only natural to mention that in a letter wouldn't it?"

"So the secret word is 'cave-in'?"

"No, let's go one step further. Make it the archaeological term, 'subsidence'. That sounds like what we'd use, don't you think?"

"Hmmm… yes it does. Right."

They exchanged a parting hug before John left to take Rosaria to dinner. They would be meeting again as soon as Victor got an audience with His Holiness.

*** 

As they drove to the Dragonara Resort, John and Rosaria discussed the success of the exhibition. It had been a long day and both had worked hard to make the occasion the success it had obviously been.

As they walked through the main entrance, John said, "I'd thought a flutter at the Casino would've been fun…"

"…But," Rosaria continued, "it'd be so much nicer to have a quiet dinner and just talk." She seemed to read his mind.

They headed for the Brasserie, and unanimously decided on dining at the Terrace Restaurant. They enjoyed each other's company as much as the excellent food.

"I can't believe," Rosaria said, "that I've only known you for a week!"

"I feel that too," John said. "You know, you remind me of someone … someone I met a long, long time ago when I was here. There was such … such beauty in her, inside and out, that I actually jumped out of my car to take a picture of her. And then … well, let's just say I've never forgotten her."

"Well, like I told you, we're all related here," she smiled gently. "I loved that poem you recited the other night. Do you have any more?"

"Well, I've written some myself."

"You write poetry? You're a poet as well?"

"No, Rose, I'm just an occasional bard," he laughed.

"Can I hear some of it? Your poetry?"

"It's just one from my earlier television appearance. I'm rather fond of it myself. It goes like this:

"If man is truly fashioned

In the image of his God,

What universal power must he possess;

## In the Image of His God

Yet for all this great potential,

As we journey through this life,

How few of us discover what we have.

If only we could realize who we are,

Could reach, not for the moon or some great star;

But could recognize within us

Lies a greatness yet unseen,

The untapped ability to fulfill our greatest dream.

The boundaries of the human mind

Are limitless like space,

A storehouse of experience and wealth;

Yet for all this great potential,

As we journey through this life,

How few of us explore our inner self.

As we move ever forward

In search of the unknown,

Striving always to prove we're not alone;

We should take the time to ponder

## PJ Shield

From whence our knowledge comes,

And to recognize within us

Beats the sound of distant drums;

Drums that speak of our creation

And our journey throughout time,

And that many of our greatest gifts

Have been forgotten in our prime;

Pushed aside and undiscovered

In our search for greater things.

Many now are rediscovered

In an academic quest,

For a greater understanding

Of the things with which we're blessed.

So give no thought unto tomorrow

As you journey on your way;

Sufficient are the problems of today

Pause now and consider

All the joys that outweigh strife,

And remember, that tomorrow

Yes, tomorrow, is the first day of the rest of your life."

Rosaria sighed deeply and then bent her head, as if in prayer. John touched her shoulder and pointed toward the sky. Together, they looked up at the star-studded night sky, reflected in the still waters of the Mediterranean. Gentle moonlight seemed to envelope the island in a mantle of protection. A memory of famous words spoken in an entirely different context tugged at John. They seemed apt for this moment. ... *This is not the end,* he thought. *It is not even the beginning of the end. But it is, perhaps, the end of the beginning.*

# Epilogue

Much had happened in the three years since he had renewed his deep friendship with Victor and met Rosaria on this magical island. Rosaria's journalistic career had been on the fast track since her paper published a series of articles on the Holy Shroud of Turin, carrying her byline. They emailed regularly, particularly drawing each other's attention to events concerning the Shroud.

Pope John Paul II died on 2 April 2005, a mere week after Victor, accompanied by John, had visited him in Rome. That last visit with the ailing pontiff had been a treasured memory for both of them.

The twenty-three mysterious deaths John had been tracking had now risen to twenty-nine. The updated report on what John always considered the 'official' shroud site at shroud.com listed them:

- *<u>March 8, 2005:</u> Raymond N. Rogers, internationally renowned chemist from Los Alamos National Laboratory and member of the Shroud of Turin Research Project (STURP) team, dies in Los Alamos, New Mexico, after a long illness.*

- *<u>April 14, 2005:</u> Paul E. Damon, professor emeritus of geosciences at the University of Arizona, and head of one of the three laboratories that performed the radiocarbon dating of the Shroud* *in 1988, suffers a stroke while working in his office and dies two days later, on April 14.*

- *April 21, 2005: Robert Dinegar, retired physicist from Los Alamos National Laboratory and member of the Shroud of Turin Research Project (STURP) team, dies in Los Alamos, New Mexico.*

- *September 11, 2005: Professor Silvano Scannerini, member of the Turin Conservation Commission on the Holy Shroud and a respected Shroud researcher, dies this date in Italy.*

- *December 14 2005: Jean Lorre, imaging expert from the Jet Propulsion Laboratory and member of the Shroud of Turin Research Project (STURP) team, dies in Pasadena, California after a brief illness.*

- *April 29, 2006: The Reverend Albert R. 'Kim' Dreisbach, Jr., Episcopal priest, founder of the Atlanta International Center for the Continuing Study of the Shroud of Turin (AICCSST), world renowned indonologist, Biblical scholar and civil rights activist, dies at the Atlanta Hartsfield Airport on his way to Italy to speak at two Shroud conferences.*

The 'curse' if that was what it was, seemed to have lifted over the last two years. *Yet here I am*, John smiled to himself, *on my way back to this wonderful island.* They were due to land in ten minutes.

Victor's last letter had included the word 'subsidence' thrice.

THE END

Printed in the United States
203827BV00001B/262-291/P